THE
BRIDGE TO
CUTTER GAP

Christy ®
of Cutter Gap

THE
BRIDGE TO CUTTER GAP

of Cutter Gap

THE SERIES

Based on the novel Christy *by*

CATHERINE MARSHALL

EVERGREEN
— FARM —

an imprint of
GILEAD PUBLISHING

The Bridge to Cutter Gap: The Christy® of Cutter Gap series
Adapted by C. Archer
Copyright © 1995 by Marshall-LeSourd, LLC

EVERGREEN
— FARM —

Published by Evergreen Farm, an imprint of Gilead Publishing, LLC,
Wheaton, Illinois, USA.
www.gileadpublishing.com/evergreenfarm

ISBN: 978-1-68370-157-6 (printed softcover)
ISBN: 978-1-68370-158-3 (ebook)

Cover design by Larry Taylor
Cover illustrations © Larry Taylor. All rights reserved.
Interior design by Beth Shagene
Ebook production by Book Genesis, Inc.

Printed in the United States of America.

18 19 20 21 22 23 24 / 5 4 3 2 1

The Characters

Christy Rudd Huddleston, a nineteen-year-old girl

Her father, mother, and brother, George

Christy's students:
    Rob Allen, fourteen
    Creed Allen, nine
    Little Burl Allen, six
    Bessie Coburn, twelve
    Vella Holt, five
    Sam Houston Holcombe, nine
    Smith O'Teale, fifteen
    Ruby May Morrison, thirteen
    John Spencer, fifteen
    Clara Spencer, twelve
    Zady Spencer, ten
    Lulu Spencer, six
    Lundy Taylor, seventeen

Scalawag, Creed Allen's pet raccoon

Alice Henderson, a Quaker mission worker from
    Ardmore, Pennsylvania

David Grantland, the young minister

Ida Grantland, David's sister

Dr. Neill MacNeill, the physician of the Cove

Jeb Spencer, a mountain man

Fairlight Spencer, his wife
(parents of Christy's students John, Clara, Zady,
and Lulu)
Their toddler, Little Guy

Bob Allen, keeper of the mill by Blackberry Creek

Mary Allen, his superstitious wife
(parents of Christy's students Rob, Creed, and
Little Burl)

Ault Allen, Bob's older brother.

Mrs. Tatum, the boarding-house lady

Ben Pentland, the mailman

Javis MacDonald, the train conductor

Dr. Ferrand, a medical missionary in the Great Smoky
Mountains

One

IT WAS HER WORST NIGHTMARE COME TRUE. SHE COULDN'T cross. She couldn't cross the bridge, not if her very life depended on it.

Christy Huddleston managed a grim smile. Bridge? It was not a bridge at all, just two huge, uneven logs with a few thin boards nailed across them here and there. A deadly layer of ice coated the logs and boards. Far below, frigid water swirled past and around and over jagged chunks of ice and razor-sharp rocks.

Christy took a step closer to the bridge. The whole contraption swayed in the biting wind. Her stomach swirled and bucked. She had never liked heights, but this . . . this was impossible.

She looked across to her guide, Ben Pentland, on the other side of the swollen creek. The mailman gazed at her doubtfully. He'd told her she wouldn't be able to make this seven-mile journey through rough, snowy terrain. "Too hard a walk for a city gal," he'd said. And now she wondered if he'd been right.

"Stomp your feet," Mr. Pentland called. "Get 'em warm. Then come on—but first scrape your boots, then hike up your skirts."

Christy hesitated. She could no longer feel her toes inside her rubber boots. Her long skirts, wet almost to her knees, were half frozen.

Mr. Pentland shook his head. "Can't get to where you're goin' without crossin' this bridge."

His words hung in the brittle air. Not for the first time that day, Christy wondered if she'd made a terrible mistake coming to this place. What was she doing here, deep in the Tennessee mountains in the middle of winter, heading off to a world she'd never seen before? Teaching school to poor mountain children had seemed like a fine idea in the cozy warmth of her home back in Asheville, North Carolina. But now . . .

She fingered the locket her father had given her before she'd left Asheville. Inside was a little picture of her parents and one of Christy and her brother, George. No one in her family had understood why she'd felt she had to come to this wild and lonely place to teach at a mission school.

And now, she wasn't so sure herself.

"Guess you ain't crossed a bridge like this before," said Mr. Pentland.

"No," Christy agreed, forcing an unsteady smile.

She took a deep breath, then put one foot on a log. It swayed a little. Her boot sent a piece of bark flying. She watched as it twirled down, falling a dozen feet to the water. The water snatched at the bit of wood and sped it away.

Another step and she was on the bridge. The sound of

the water became a roar in her ears. There was no turning back now.

"You're doin' fine," came Mr. Pentland's soothing voice. "Keep a-comin'. Not far now."

Not far now? It seemed he was a hundred miles away, safe on the far side.

The logs swayed and tilted. Christy stared at her feet as she struggled with her heavy, wet dress. Another step. Another. With great effort, she forced herself to look at Mr. Pentland.

She was halfway there. She was going to make it.

Another step, and another. The far side was—

Her boot slid on a crosspiece. She clutched at empty air for support that was not there, slipped, and landed hard on her knees. She clung as best she could to the icy log.

Mr. Pentland was shouting something and coming out to her. She crawled another few inches toward him.

Why am I here, risking my life to get to a place I've never seen? some sensible part of herself kept asking. *Why is teaching so important to me?* Had it only been yesterday that she'd stepped aboard the train to Tennessee, so confident and full of hope? Christy's mind raced as she slowly crawled toward Mr. Pentland.

Her right knee hit a slick spot on the log, and her weight shifted. Slowly—terrifyingly slowly—she slid over the side of the bridge.

"No!" she cried. She clawed for support, but her fingers lost their grip. She was falling, falling, toward the icy creek below. The roar of the water and the sound of her own screams filled her ears, and as she fell she wondered why she had to die now, die here—when she was trying to do something so good.

As the icy waters rushed over her, the events of the last two days flashed across Christy's mind. Was this the way it would end?

Two

One day earlier

"Now, you watch your step going out to the car. With all that snow last night, the walk's bound to be icy." Mrs. Huddleston fussed with the bow of her crisp white apron. Tears glistened in her eyes.

Christy took a deep breath to keep herself from crying too. The look of love and longing in her mother's eyes was hard to bear. "I'll be careful," she promised.

Slowly, Christy took in the smells and sights around her, all the things she was leaving behind for who knew how long. The smell of starch in her mother's apron, the hissing of the pine resin in the big iron stove in the kitchen, and the sleepy half smile on George's face. Her brother had stumbled out of bed just in time to see Christy off.

"We have to go," Mr. Huddleston repeated from the doorway. "The engine's running. I had a time cranking the car in this cold."

Mrs. Huddleston took Christy's hands in her own. "You're sure about this?" she whispered.

"Positive," Christy said.

"Promise me you'll take care of yourself."

"I promise. Really I do."

After a flurry of hugs and kisses, Christy settled at last into the front seat of the car. Her father drove silently, intent on navigating the icy roads. Asheville was a hilly town, and driving took all his concentration as he made his way in the predawn gloom to the railroad station.

In the gray light, the station had a ghostly look. Black smoke billowed from the engine smokestack as Mr. Huddleston parked and they climbed out. The slamming of the car doors seemed unnaturally loud and final.

Christy began the walk to the train, keeping pace beside her father. She tensed, waiting for what she knew would come. She'd battled long and hard with her parents for the chance to leave home like this. At nineteen, they considered her far too young to be going off alone on a wild adventure like teaching school in the Tennessee mountains. She'd told them that she was grown-up now. That this was, after all, 1912, and that women could take advantage of all kinds of exciting opportunities. Her life in Asheville was nothing but teas and receptions and ladies' polite talk, dance parties, and picnics in the summer. A good enough life, certainly. But she knew in her heart that there had to be more than that waiting for her somewhere. All she had to do was find it.

Her parents had argued with her, pleaded, bargained. But Christy was stubborn, like all the Huddlestons, and this time she was the one who'd gotten her way. She'd been thrilled at her victory too—that is, until now, looking at her father's worried, gentle face, and his too gray hair.

"My hand's cold," she said suddenly, sticking her fingers

into the pocket of his overcoat. It was a childish gesture, but her father understood. He paused, smiling at her sadly.

"Girlie," he said, using his favorite nickname for her, "do you really think you have enough money to get you through till payday?" His breath frosted in the crisp January air.

"Plenty, Father."

"Twenty-five dollars a month isn't going to go far."

"It'll be good for me," Christy said lightly. "For the first time in my life, I probably won't have the chance to shop."

Reaching into his other pocket, Mr. Huddleston retrieved a small package. It was wrapped in blue paper and tied with a satin bow.

"Father!" Christy exclaimed. "For me?"

"It's nothing, really," he said, clearing his throat. "From your mother and me."

Christy fumbled with the wrapping. Inside sat a black velvet-covered box. She opened it to discover a heart-shaped silver locket.

"Great-grandmother's necklace!" Christy cried.

"Go ahead," her father said. "Open it."

With trembling fingers, Christy opened the tiny engraved heart. Inside were two pictures. One was a carefully posed photograph of her parents: her mother with a gentle smile, her father gazing sternly at the camera with just a hint of a smile in the creases of his eyes. On the other side was a picture of Christy and her brother, taken last summer at their church retreat.

"That's so you won't forget us," her father said with a wink.

"Oh, Father," Christy said, wiping away a tear, "as if I ever could!"

Her father helped her put on the necklace, then led her

to the steps of the train. She climbed aboard and gazed with interest at the brass spittoons, at the potbellied stove in the rear, at the faces of the other passengers. It was only a few hours to El Pano, the stop nearest to Christy's new job, but it felt as if she were about to embark on a journey around the world. She had taken train trips before, of course, but never alone. This time everything seemed new, perhaps because she was going away without knowing when she would return.

Christy sank down onto a scratchy red-plush seat and smiled up at her father, who had followed her on board. He placed her suitcase on the floor beside her. The whistle blew shrilly.

"Don't forget now," her father said. "Soon as you get there, write us." He gave her an awkward hug, and then he was gone. Out on the platform, Christy saw him talking to the old conductor. Mr. Huddleston pointed in her direction, and Christy sighed. She knew what he was saying: "Take good care of my girl." It was embarrassing. After all, if she was old enough to go off on this adventure, she was old enough to take care of herself on the train. And the train was going to be the easy part of this trip.

"All a-boarrrd!" the conductor called. The engine wheezed. *Chuff . . . chuff . . . chuff.* The train jerked forward, and a moment later the telephone poles outside began sliding past. Before long, the conductor was making his way down the aisle, gathering tickets.

Please, Christy thought desperately, *don't humiliate me in front of the other passengers. I'm a big girl. I can take care of myself.*

"Ticket, please," came the old man's voice. "You're Christy Huddleston, aren't you?"

Christy nodded, trying her best to seem like a dignified adult.

"I'm Javis MacDonald. I've known your father a long time," the conductor said as he punched her ticket. "So you're bound for El Pano, young lady. I understand you'll be teaching school there?"

"No, actually I'll be teaching in Cutter Gap," Christy corrected. "It's a few miles out of El Pano."

Mr. MacDonald rubbed his whiskers. His expression grew troubled. "That Cutter Gap is rough country," he said. "Last week during a turkey-shooting match, one man got tired of shooting turkeys. Shot another man in the back instead."

Christy felt a shiver skate down her spine, but she kept the same even smile on her face. *Is Cutter Gap really such a dangerous place?*

The conductor gazed at Christy with the same worried look she'd seen on her parents' faces this morning. "I suppose I shouldn't be telling you that sort of thing. But you'll be seeing it for yourself soon enough. It's a hard place, Cutter Gap."

"I'm sure I'll be fine," Christy said.

"If you were my daughter, I'd send you home on the first train back. That's no place for a girl like you."

A girl like me, Christy thought, her cheeks blazing. What did that mean anyway? What kind of girl was she? Maybe that was why she'd started on this trip: to find out who she was and where her place was in the world.

As the conductor moved on, she opened her locket. The sight of her parents brought tears to her eyes. George gazed back at her with his usual I'm-about-to-cause-trouble grin. But it was her own picture that caught her attention.

The slender, almost girlish figure and the blue eyes beneath piled-up dark hair.

What was it in her eyes? A question? A glimmer of understanding? Of hope? Of searching?

That picture had been taken at the end of the church retreat last summer. By then, she'd decided that she had to go to Cutter Gap. The answers to her questions lay somewhere in the Great Smoky Mountains.

It seemed strange that she'd found a clue about where her life might go from a perfect stranger rather than from her own family or her church back in Asheville. But the elderly little man who'd spoken to the retreat group with such passion had reached her in a way no one else ever had. Dr. Ferrand was a medical doctor doing mission work in the Great Smokies. He'd spoken of the need for volunteers to help teach and care for the mountain people—or highlanders, as he'd called them. He'd talked of desperate poverty and ignorance. He'd told the story of a boy, Rob Allen, who wanted book learning so much that he walked to school barefoot through six-foot snow.

Listening to his moving words, Christy had glanced down at her pointed, buttoned shoes with their black, patent-leather tops—the shoes she'd bought just the week before. Thinking of the barefoot boy, she'd felt a shudder of guilt. She had known there was poverty in places like Africa and China, but was it possible that such awful conditions existed a train's ride away from her home town?

Dr. Ferrand went on to talk about someone who shared his passion to help the mountain people: Miss Alice Henderson, a Quaker from Ardmore, Pennsylvania, and a new breed of woman who had braved hardship and danger to serve where she saw need.

I would like to know that woman, Christy thought. *I would like to live my life that way.*

By the time they sang the closing hymn, "Just As I Am," Christy felt herself coming to a very important decision. Her heart welled up so full she could hardly sing the words.

When the benediction was over, she made her way down the aisle to Dr. Ferrand. "You asked for volunteers," Christy said. "You're looking at one. I can teach anywhere you want to use me." She was not the most well-educated girl in the world, but she knew she could teach children to read.

A long silence fell. The little man gazed at her doubtfully. "Are you sure, my child?"

"Quite sure."

And so it was done. There had been plenty of arguments with her parents. But for the first time in her life, Christy Rudd Huddleston had felt certain she was about to take the world by storm. Even her parents' disapproval couldn't change her mind. After all, she'd told herself, throughout history the many men and women who had accomplished great things must have had to shrug off other people's opinions too.

Suddenly the train screeched to a halt. The conductor's gruff voice broke into Christy's thoughts. "A snowdrift has flung two big rocks onto the roadbed, folks," he said. "There's a train crew comin' to clear the tracks. Shouldn't take long."

At the rear of the coach, the potbellied stove was smoking. Across the aisle, a woman was changing the diaper of her red-faced and squalling baby.

A little fresh air couldn't hurt, Christy thought. She buttoned her coat, reached for her muff, and headed outside.

Snowflakes as big as goose feathers were still falling. As far as she looked, she could see nothing but mountain peak piled upon mountain peak. It was a lonely landscape—lonelier still when the wind rose suddenly, making a sad, sobbing sound. It was a wind with pain in it.

Christy shivered. Was she going to be homesick even before she reached her destination?

She returned to the coach. A long time passed before the train once again chugged slowly toward its destination. Outside, as the sun sank, the world glittered with ice, turning every bush and withered blade of grass to jewels—sapphires and turquoise, emeralds and rubies and diamonds.

Darkness came suddenly as, for what seemed like the thousandth time, Christy imagined her welcome at the train station. Someone would, of course, be sent to meet her—a welcoming committee of some kind.

"Miss Huddleston?" they would ask. "Are you the new teacher for the mission?" They would look her over, and their eyes would say, "We were expecting a young girl, but you're a grown woman!"

At last the train began to slow and Mr. MacDonald announced they were coming into El Pano. As he lighted the railroad lanterns on the floor in front of the coach, the engine's wheels ground to a stop. Christy reached for her muff and suitcase and started down the aisle. She was certain she could hear the nervous beating of her own heart.

"Let me help you with that suitcase," the conductor said. "Easy on those steps. They may be slippery."

Christy stepped down to the ground. Her eyes searched the dark. There wasn't much to see—just the tiny station and four or five houses. Where was the welcoming committee she'd imagined?

A few men came out of the little station and began to unload boxes from a baggage cart. Now and then they paused to stare at Christy, muttering and laughing under their breath.

"You're a mighty pert young woman, Miss Huddleston," said the conductor. "But land sakes—watch yourself out there at Cutter Gap."

"Thank you," Christy said, trying to sound confident despite the fear rising in her. She spun around, searching again for some sign that she was not about to be left completely alone. But no one was coming. The snowy landscape lay deserted.

"It's not too late to change your mind," Mr. MacDonald said as he climbed the train steps.

Christy just gave him a smile and a wave. Slowly the train began to move. The smaller it grew, the greater the lump in Christy's throat. And then, from a distance, the engine whistle blew. Her heart clutched at the sound.

Finally, there was nothing but emptiness. She was alone. All alone.

The men finished unloading the baggage cart. She could feel their eyes on her, hear their whispers. With a firm grip on her suitcase, Christy strode toward the little station. Whatever happened, from this moment on, this was her adventure.

She was not about to let anyone see how afraid she really was.

Three

INSIDE THE LITTLE STATION, A GROUP OF MEN STOOD NEAR the stove. They fell silent as Christy headed toward the grilled window where the ticket agent stood.

"Sir?" Christy said to the old man. He did not look up. "Could you tell me if there's somewhere in town where I could spend the night?"

There was no answer.

"Sir," Christy repeated loudly. "Could you tell me—"

"Young woman, you'll have to speak up."

This time Christy practically shouted her question. The men near the stove laughed loudly.

"Well, now," said the ticket agent. "Let's see. Maybe Miz Tatum's."

"Where is that?"

"Oh, close. You just—" he paused and shook his head— "Guess it's easier to show you."

Christy followed the man back out into the stinging cold.

He pointed across the tracks. "Can't quite make it out, but it's that big house, second one down. You'll find it."

Christy nodded, peering into the velvety darkness.

"Just tell Miz Tatum that I sent you. You'll get plenty to eat and a clean bed." He chuckled. "Mind you, Miz Tatum can talk the hind legs off a donkey."

Christy soon discovered that carrying a heavy suitcase wasn't easy, not while holding up long skirts at the same time. Halfway to the boarding house, she slipped and fell. The snow churning up over her shoe tops was bad enough, but the laughter coming from the old ticket agent was even worse.

Mustering as much dignity as she could, Christy struggled to her feet and made her way toward the Victorian frame house the agent had pointed out. Yellow lamplight glowed from several windows, and smoke poured out of both chimneys. The cozy sight filled her with a sudden, desperate longing for her own home back in Asheville. Her parents and George would be sitting down to supper right about now. She could almost hear her father's soft voice saying grace.

Christy set her suitcase on the porch, shook out her snowy skirts, and twirled the bell. Once more she glanced around her, hoping for a sight of the welcoming committee she'd imagined in such detail. But the street lay empty and perfectly silent. The whole world seemed to be holding its breath.

A tall, big-boned woman opened the door. "Yes?"

"Mrs. Tatum?" Christy asked.

The woman nodded, arms crossed over her chest.

"I'm Christy Huddleston from Asheville. The station man told me you take in roomers. Could I rent a room?"

"Sure could. Come on in out of the cold. Bad night, ain't it?"

"Yes, it is," Christy agreed, filled with relief. For tonight, at least, she would have a place to stay.

As Christy stepped inside, the woman looked her over carefully. "You come from Asheville way?" she said, taking Christy's suitcase. "Not many women come through here on the train. Where you bound?"

"I—" Christy began.

"Oh, but listen to me!" Mrs. Tatum interrupted. "There's time enough for questions. Let me show you to your room, child." She pointed to a lamp. "Bring that lamp over there."

The room upstairs was plain and clean. A shiny brass bed sat in the center. "Now, you make yourself at home," Mrs. Tatum instructed, setting down Christy's suitcase. Once again she gazed, eyes full of questions. "I'll build up the fire downstairs, and you can eat by the stove."

Before Christy could respond, Mrs. Tatum was bustling out the door. Christy changed clothes quickly, shivering in the unheated room. A nice, hot fire would be a welcome relief. Her toes were practically numb.

She picked up the lamp and groped her way down the dark stairs to the kitchen.

Mrs. Tatum had put on a large calico apron. "Here's your supper," she said as Christy sat at the kitchen table. "Spareribs and pickled beans. And there's some sourwood honey and some apple butter to put on the biscuit bread. I saved the sourwood honey for something special."

"Thank you," Christy said, suddenly realizing how hungry she was.

"So tell me now," Mrs. Tatum said, watching as Christy began to eat, "where exactly are you bound?"

Christy swallowed a piece of biscuit bread. "I've come to teach school at the mission. You know—out at Cutter Gap."

Mrs. Tatum practically gasped. "Land sakes, child. You,

teaching? At Cutter Gap? What does your mama think about that?"

"Oh, it's all right with my parents," Christy said, not wanting to discuss that whole thing. "After all, I am nineteen."

Mrs. Tatum settled into a chair next to Christy. "Have they seen Cutter Gap?" she asked, eyes wide.

"No," Christy admitted. *Do all middle-aged people think this way?* she wondered silently.

"Look," Mrs. Tatum said sincerely. "I just don't think you know what you're getting yourself into. I'm a pretty good judge of folks, and it's easy to tell you come from a fancy home—your clothes, the way you talk."

"My home isn't that fancy," Christy protested. "Besides, I'm not afraid of plain living."

"Mercy sakes alive! You don't know how plain. Did you ever have to sleep in a bed with the quilts held down by rocks just to keep the wind from blowing the covers off?"

Christy smiled. Surely Mrs. Tatum was exaggerating.

"The thing is I know those mountain people." Mrs. Tatum lowered her voice. "They don't take much stock in foreigners."

"What do you mean, foreigners?" Christy protested. "I'm an American citizen, born in the Smoky Mountains."

"Now, don't get riled," Mrs. Tatum soothed. "The folks in Cutter Gap think anyone who's not from there is a foreigner. They're mighty proud people. It's going to be well-nigh impossible for you to help them."

Christy pushed back her plate. As much as Mrs. Tatum's words bothered her, she didn't want to show it. *"She could talk the hind legs off a donkey,"* the station man had said. Was this just so much talk?

"That was excellent," Christy said, hoping to change the subject. "Thank you, Mrs. Tatum. I was starving."

Mrs. Tatum reached for Christy's plate. Her brow furrowed. "Look, maybe you don't like somebody like me that you never saw before tonight butting in. But my advice is that you get yourself on the next train and go straight back to your folks."

How could I run away like that, before I've even seen Cutter Gap? Christy wondered as she pushed back her chair and stood.

"Mrs. Tatum," she said gently, "I've given my word about teaching school. A promise is a promise." She reached for the lamp. "How far is the Gap from here, anyway?"

"Seven miles, more or less."

"How can I get out there tomorrow?"

Mrs. Tatum clucked her tongue. "My, you are eager, aren't you?" She sighed. "Ben Pentland carries the mail out that way, but he ain't been there since the snow fell."

"How could I talk to Mr. Pentland?"

"At the general store most likely, come morning."

"Thanks again for the supper, Mrs. Tatum. And please don't worry about me."

Christy glanced over her shoulder as she started up the stairs. Mrs. Tatum was staring at her, shaking her head in disapproval.

Back in her cold bedroom, Christy stared out the window at the little village beyond. The houses were roofed with silver, the railroad tracks a pair of shining ribbons. Where was Cutter Gap from here? Was it really such an awful place? What if her parents were right? Her parents and the conductor and

Mrs. Tatum . . . What if they were all right? Didn't anyone think she was doing the right thing, coming here?

They need a teacher, Christy told herself. Dr. Ferrand had said they were desperate for help. But then why hadn't anyone been here to greet her? Had he forgotten to tell them she was coming? No, she had a letter from him. It couldn't be that.

Cold air seeped through the window. Christy retreated to the dresser and began to pull hairpins from her hair. She stared at her reflection in the mirror. Staring back was a face too thin, too angular. For the millionth time she wished she were beautiful, like her friend Eileen back in Asheville. She sighed. Her eyes were too big for the rest of her face. But this time she saw something new in them—something she'd never seen before.

She saw fear.

She opened her suitcase. Digging through the layers of clothing—she hadn't been sure what to bring, so she'd brought a little of everything—she found what she was looking for. Clutching the leather-bound diary to her chest, she leapt under the covers, grateful for the warmth of Mrs. Tatum's old quilt. She opened to the first, crisp page, yellow in the lamplight. Her fountain pen poised, she waited for the perfect words to come to her. This was, after all, the beginning of her adventure. She'd promised herself she would write it all down—good and bad, highs and lows.

January 7, 1912
My trip to El Pano was uneventful.

Christy wrote in her pretty, swirling handwriting. She stared at the words, then smiled at herself. *Be honest, Christy,* she told herself.

She tapped the fountain pen against her chin.

*I have begun my great adventure this day, and
although things have not gone exactly as I had hoped, I
am still committed to my dream of teaching at the mission.*

*The day began with a heavy snowfall, which has made
for difficult travel. Last night when it began to snow,
Mother said, jokingly, that perhaps I should take it as an
omen.*

*I don't believe in such things, of course. Neither does
Mother. (I suppose she was just hoping to convince me not
to go, although she knew in her heart that was not to be.)*

*Still, upon my arrival in El Pano, no one was here to
greet me, and I cannot help but wonder if that is not a
bad sign. I want to be wanted, I suppose. To feel that my
coming here is a good thing.*

*The truth is I have not been this afraid before or felt
this alone and homesick. Leaving everyone I love was
harder than I thought it would be. But I must be strong. I
am at the start of a great adventure. And great adventures
are sometimes scary.*

Christy set her pen and diary on the night table. She lay
back with a sigh and pulled the covers up to her neck.

It was a long, long time before she finally fell into a rest-
less sleep.

Four

She was having that dream again. She knew it was a dream, because she'd had it so many times.

She was standing on the railroad trestle, two hundred feet above the French Broad River. She and some friends had been on a picnic, and now they were heading home across the bridge. Her friends urged her on, but every time Christy looked down at the open spaces beneath her feet, her stomach began to somersault, and her head turned to the rushing noise like the river raging far below her.

She looked down, down through the hole to her certain death, and her knees became liquid. Someone screamed, and then she was falling, falling, falling . . .

Christy's eyes flew open. A dream. It was just a dream, the same dream she'd had a million times before. She tried to swallow. Her throat was tight, her skin damp with sweat.

If it were just a dream, why did it feel so real this time?

She blinked. In the early morning light, she took in the surroundings of Mrs. Tatum's guest room. It was so cold that Christy's breath formed little clouds.

She glanced at her diary on the night table beside her bed. It was still open to the page where she'd begun writing. *"I have not been this afraid before,"* she read.

Well, no wonder her dreams were getting the better of her. Yesterday had been quite a day. She stared out the window at the snowy, mountainous landscape. Somewhere out there, Cutter Gap was waiting for her.

Today, she vowed, would go more smoothly.

⟨⁓⟩

When she pushed open the door to the general store, Christy was greeted by the smells of coal oil, strong cheese, leather, bacon fat, and tobacco. A group of men sat by the stove, whittling and rocking and talking among themselves. At the nearest counter, a woman arranged spools of thread in a cabinet under curving glass.

"Excuse me," Christy said. "I was told I might find Mr. Pentland, the mailman, here."

The woman's eyes swept the men. "Ben," she called loudly, "come here, will you?"

A man looked up from the high boots he was lacing. When he stood, he unfolded like a jackknife to a height of over six feet. He was wearing overalls covered by a frayed and unpressed suit coat. But it was his face that caught Christy's attention—long and slim, creased by wind and weather, with bushy, arching eyebrows and deep-set eyes that sparkled.

"This here's Ben Pentland," said the woman. "Miss—"

Christy stuck out a mittened hand. "Christy Huddleston from Asheville."

"Howdy." He took her hand so firmly that she winced.

"You're the postman, aren't you?"

"Yep."

Obviously, Mr. Pentland was a man of few words. Christy glanced back at the circle of men watching her and Mr. Pentland with clear curiosity.

"Could I talk with you a minute?" Christy asked. "Back there, maybe?"

Mr. Pentland followed Christy toward the back of the store where the hardware and the harnesses and saddles were kept. "Mr. Pentland, I need help," she said. "I've come to teach school in Cutter Gap. I thought someone would meet me at the station yesterday, but nobody did. So I'm trying to find a way to get there. Mrs. Tatum said you could help me since you carry the mail out that way."

"Yep," he said proudly. "Carry the letters regular. But ain't nobody been in or out of Cutter Gap in a couple days. Snow's too deep."

"When are you going next?"

"Startin' now. That's why I was gettin' my boots on. Letters are piled up somethin' fearful."

"Do you ride?"

The mailman looked astonished at her question. "No critter could make it in this snow!"

Christy felt her heart sink a little. Mrs. Tatum had said it was seven miles from here to Cutter Gap. Christy had never walked seven miles at one stretch in her entire life. But what did that matter? She couldn't exactly sit here waiting for the snow to melt and spring to come.

"Could I walk out there with you today?" Christy asked.

"Nope. Too hard a walk for a city gal. These here mountains make for tough walking, and the deep snow makes it near impossible, even for mountain people. And besides, you're just a runt of a girl. You'd never make it."

He did not sound like he was going to change his mind. "Mr. Pentland," Christy said forcefully, "you don't understand. I'm strong, honestly I am, and the snow may last for weeks."

"Sorry, miss. It just wouldn't be right for a woman to go along with the U-nited States mail." He took a step back and placed his hand over his heart, as if he was about to salute the flag. "'Neither rain . . . nor snow . . . nor heat . . . nor gloom of night . . . will stay these couriers from the swift completion of their appointed rounds.'"

Christy stared at him in amazement. She had never heard that slogan before. Was Mr. Pentland making fun of her?

"Beautiful, ain't it?" Mr. Pentland asked. "The government in Washington wrote it up for us. Anyway, I figure if rain or snow can't stop us from getting the mail where it needs to go, then I surely can't have no city gal getting in the way." He turned to rejoin his companions by the stove.

Now what? Mr. Pentland was Christy's only chance to get to Cutter Gap. She couldn't give up, not yet.

"Mr. Pentland, please," Christy begged, running after him. "That's a wonderful slogan. I promise I won't interfere with the mail one bit. I won't even slow you down. Please? At least consider it?"

The mailman looked her over doubtfully. "Look, I don't want to discourage you, but it's for your own good. It ain't easy, walkin' in the snow. And what about your things?"

So he was weakening—at least a little. "I only have one small suitcase," Christy said hopefully. "The rest of my things are being shipped in a trunk. May I—" she smiled her most winning smile. "May I come with you?"

Mr. Pentland shook his head, then grinned back. "Can you be ready in a hip and a hurry?"

"Ten minutes," Christy vowed.

She ran back to Mrs. Tatum's and quickly gathered her belongings together. As she said goodbye on the front porch, Mrs. Tatum took Christy's face between her hands, kissing first one cheek and then the other.

"That's for your mother, since she ain't here," she said. "And you let her know that I did my level best to send you home to her." She shook her head. "You're a sight on the eyes. They've never seen the likes of you before, out at the mission." She thrust a brown paper bag into Christy's hand. "No use walkin' on an empty stomach."

Christy turned to see Mr. Pentland, waiting impatiently by the edge of the road. "Women!" he muttered under his breath, clearly embarrassed by all the female fuss. "Always cacklin' like hens!"

"I must go," Christy said. "Thank you again for everything, Mrs. Tatum."

"Mind you watch that slippery log bridge over the creek!" Mrs. Tatum warned. "The Lord bless you and keep you, child."

⟀

Mr. Pentland walked at a brisk pace, but Christy managed to keep up with him. She was feeling much more hopeful this morning. The world looked fresh and welcoming, coated with glistening snow. Over the far mountains a soft smoky-blue haze hung like a cloak, but in the valley where she was walking the sky was clear blue.

Things were definitely looking up, Christy decided. Not only was Mr. Pentland letting her tag along, but he had even offered to carry her suitcase along with his mail bag. Out here, surrounded by the beauty of the mountains, the warnings she'd been hearing about Cutter Gap seemed silly.

After a while, Mr. Pentland turned and gave Christy a smile. "Maybe I should whittle down my walk a bit," he said. "Women's skirts ain't the best for snow."

Christy smiled back. There was something courteous and dignified about Mr. Pentland that she liked. His speech was full of odd expressions she had never heard before. The sun was a "sunball." Twilight was "the edge of dark." A mountain lion was a "painter." The words were beautiful but very strange to her ears.

"Mr. Pentland," Christy asked as they began to walk more slowly, "how many families are there in Cutter Gap?"

He thought for a moment. "Maybe 'bout seventy in the Cove," he answered at last.

"'The Cove'?" Christy repeated.

"A cove is like a holler."

Christy shook her head, still confused.

"You know, a valley, between them mountains."

"Oh!" Christy nodded, understanding dawning at last. Would it always be so hard, she wondered, communicating with these people? "Most of the people farm, don't they?" she asked. "What crops? What do they raise?"

"Raise youngsters, mostly," he answered dryly.

Christy couldn't help smiling. "And do most of these children go to the mission school?"

"Well, now, that depends. Not all of them has got religion. 'Course, most everyone seems to like the new preacher, David Grantland."

"Has he been at the mission long?"

"Three months or so."

"What else can you tell me about him? Is he married?"

Mr. Pentland looked at Christy and chuckled. "Nope," he said.

Christy felt a blush rising in her cheeks. "Tell me," she said, quickly changing the subject, "do you know Miss Alice Henderson?"

"Everybody in Cutter Gap knows Miz Henderson."

"What's she like? What does she look like?"

The mountaineer shifted Christy's suitcase to his other hand, considering her questions. "Well, she's a smiley woman. All her wrinkles are smile wrinkles. Keeps busier than a honeybee 'round a rosebush. Started two schools and churches before comin' to Cutter Gap, she did. She rides a horse all over the mountains by herself. Sidesaddle, long skirt. Teachin', preachin', nursin' the sick, comfortin' the dyin'." He smiled. "She has a heap of hair. Wears it in braids 'round her head, like a crown. And she sits in that saddle like a queen."

Christy considered the picture he'd painted for her. Because of his speech and the fact that he hadn't had much formal education, she'd jumped to the conclusion that Mr. Pentland was a simple man. Clearly she'd been wrong. That was something she needed to remember.

Mr. Pentland stopped at a small, rustic cabin, calling out, "Mornin'! U-nited States mail!"

A woman rushed out to retrieve her two precious letters, waving happily at Mr. Pentland.

"How many more stops will we have?" Christy asked as they headed on.

"Four more letters. Ain't that a wonder!"

"But back at the store you said—" Christy stopped

midsentence, trying to understand this mountain world where six letters meant "piled-up" mail.

Soon the trail grew so winding and narrow that they had to walk single file. After a couple of hours of tramping in Mr. Pentland's footsteps, the cold had begun to creep into Christy's bones. Her eyes stung. Her skirts were wet from snow and were beginning to stiffen in the cold. Her eyelashes were beaded with wet snow.

As she trudged along, she began to wonder if she really could make it all seven miles. She hadn't imagined that the trail would be so steep. And what was that Mrs. Tatum had said about the "slippery log bridge"? Whatever she'd meant, it didn't sound easy.

Gradually the path grew almost vertical. The trail seemed to have been sliced out of the side of the mountain to their right. To their left, the ledge dropped off into space. Before long, it was five hundred feet to the valley floor below. Christy's breath came in short, hard gasps.

"This here's Lonesome Pine Ridge," Mr. Pentland called back. "There's another way that's shorter. But that way is so uptilted you could stand up straight and bite the ground."

Struggling for breath, Christy wondered silently if any piece of land could be more uptilted than this. The wind grew fiercer, a gale from the north with a howl that stood her hair on end. The closer they got to the top of the ridge, the more certain she was that she would be blown right over the cliff, falling to a rocky death.

The memory of the falling dream—the one she'd had last night—came back to her suddenly. She shivered, but she couldn't tell if it was from fear or from the never-ending, bitter-cold wind that seemed to sneak its way inside her coat. She studied her feet. One foot in front of the other. One dainty boot into each of Mr. Pentland's great footprints. She was beginning to see why the mailman hadn't wanted her to come. This morning seemed like days and days ago.

Don't think about the wind, Christy told herself. *Don't think about how high you are. You are having an adventure, a great and wonderful adventure.*

Mr. Pentland must have sensed she was afraid. He called back over his shoulder, "Not much farther now to the Spencers' cabin. They live just on the other side. Guess we could stop and sit a spell by their fire and let you warm yourself."

"I'd like that," Christy called back wearily.

"You must be mighty tired out," Mr. Pentland called. "It's just another step or two."

At last, when Christy didn't think she could go another foot, they came upon a cabin made of rough logs chinked together with mud. In the cleared place enclosed by a split-rail fence sat an immense black pot, a tall pile of logs for firewood, and some squawking chickens pecking in the snow.

A man wearing overalls and a large, black felt hat appeared on the porch. "Howdy!" he called. Hounds raced toward Mr. Pentland and Christy, wagging their tails and yapping happily.

"Howdy," Mr. Pentland called back. "Jeb Spencer, this here's Miz Huddleston. New teacher from Asheville."

"Howdy-do, ma'am," the man said respectfully.

He led them through the doorway into the gloomy little cabin. At first Christy could see nothing but the red glow of firelight. Then she noticed several beds piled high with quilts. In the shadows to one side stood a tall woman and an assortment of children, all of them with white-blond hair.

"Come and see the new teacher," Mr. Spencer said to the children. He nodded at the woman in the shadows. "This here's my wife, Fairlight," he explained to Christy. "And that's Zady, Clara, Lulu." He pointed to a tiny boy. "And that there is Little Guy. The oldest boy, John, he's out huntin'."

Would these children soon be some of my students? Christy wondered. She smiled at them and held her hand out to Mrs. Spencer. But the pretty woman didn't seem to know what to do. She touched Christy's fingers shyly. "Would you like to sit a spell?" she asked softly in a sweet, musical voice.

Christy could scarcely take her eyes off Fairlight Spencer. She was beautiful, in a plain, simple way. She had on a worn calico dress and her feet were bare, despite the cold.

The Spencers, Christy realized, were watching her just as closely. As she took off her coat, the children seemed to be fascinated with the red sweater she wore underneath.

Mr. Pentland handed Mrs. Spencer the lunch Mrs. Tatum had prepared. "You must be starvin'," the woman said softly. "Dinner'll be on the table right quick. You two rest up."

While Christy held her hands close to the fire, she had a better chance to look around the cabin. It was just two rooms, side by side. This one, she guessed, judging from all the beds, must serve as both the living and sleeping quarters. The other was the kitchen.

The children's bright eyes were still watching Christy. The littlest girl, the one named Lulu, had the fat-cheeked cherub look of a china doll. The tiny toddler—the one his father had called Little Guy—came up and touched his shy fingers to Christy's red sweater.

After a few minutes, Mrs. Spencer called everyone to dinner. The whole group gathered around a plank table set in a

corner near the kitchen. Mr. Spencer began asking the bless-
ing in a loud, clear voice. "Thank Thee, Lord, for providin'
this bounty. Bless us and bind us. Amen."

Just then, out of the corner of her eye, Christy noticed a
small gray pig.

As soon as the amen had been spoken, the older girl
named Clara spoke up eagerly. "That there's Belinda, our pet
pig," she said proudly. She picked up the pig and set it in her
lap.

Christy tried not to show her surprise. But she couldn't
help thinking that a smelly pig at the table was probably just
the beginning of what she'd have to get used to here in the
mountains. And after all, her mother had always insisted that
a lady should be poised under all circumstances. If only her
mother could see—not to mention smell—this house. Were
all the homes in Cutter Gap as primitive as this one?

Mrs. Spencer placed a big black pot of steaming cabbage
on the table, and the men broke up cornbread to sop it up. It
looked awful to Christy. Longingly she gazed at Mrs. Tatum's
ham sandwiches, which Mrs. Spencer had placed on a tin
plate. The children were staring at them with total fascination.

"Would you like one of my sandwiches?" Christy asked,
and within seconds they had disappeared. Even Belinda the
pig sneaked a small bite.

Taking a piece of cornbread, Christy gazed at the
unscrubbed faces around her. There was something strong
and serious about them—something that reflected a spirit
and attitude from a time long ago. It was as if one of those old
tintype photographs of pioneers had come to life. *Well, these
are pioneers, in a way,* she thought. It certainly had taken
strength and courage to journey hundreds of miles through

wilderness to settle here. And it would take strength indeed to live and try to keep house in a cabin like this one.

Sitting there with these people, Christy had a strange feeling. It was as if, in crossing the mountains with Mr. Pentland, she had crossed into another time, back to the days of the American frontier. Was she still Christy Rudd Huddleston from Asheville, North Carolina? Or was she somebody else? It was as if the pages of her history book had opened—as if, by some magic, Daniel Boone or Davy Crockett could walk into this cabin at any moment. But this was no storybook. This was real.

"Are you likin' the food all right?" Fairlight Spencer asked nervously.

Just as Christy opened her mouth to answer, a little red-haired boy rushed into the cabin. He leaned against the chimney, gasping for breath.

"Creed Allen!" Mrs. Spencer cried. "What on earth is it?"

"Mighty sorry, Miz Spencer," he gasped. "But Pa's been hurt bad! It was a fallin' tree. Hit him on the head!"

"Where is he?" Mr. Spencer asked.

"They're carrying him here." The little boy's eyes fell on Christy. "He was on his way to the station to fetch the new teacher when it happened!"

Five

CHRISTY GASPED, THE BOY'S WORDS WHIRLING IN HER head. So that was why no one had been at the station to meet her. A horrible feeling of guilt swept over her. Someone had been hurt because of her.

A moment later, two boys carried in a makeshift stretcher made of branches. A man lay on it, limp and unconscious. His head was bloody. Mr. Spencer took one end of the stretcher and helped the boys ease the injured man onto a bed. Mrs. Spencer removed the man's heavy shoes and covered him with a quilt.

This happened because of me, Christy thought. She stared at the breathless little boy kneeling by the bed. "Pa," he'd said. This poor man, so badly hurt, was the boy's father.

"Is Doc comin'?" Mr. Spencer asked.

"Yep," one of the boys answered. "Ought to be here pretty quick."

"Who is the man who's hurt?" Christy managed to whisper to Mrs. Spencer.

"That be Bob Allen." Her voice was gentle, as if she sensed

how Christy felt. "Miz Henderson asked Bob to fetch you at the station. But it was probably snowin' too heavy on Sunday for him to journey. Guess he figured the snow had you stuck there." She nodded at one of the boys who'd carried in the stretcher. He was tall and slender, about fourteen or so. "That be Rob Allen, Bob's oldest son."

Christy thought for a moment. Hadn't that been the name of the boy Dr. Ferrand had mentioned in his speech last summer? The boy who had walked to school for miles, barefoot, because he was so anxious to learn?

Christy glanced at the boy's feet. They were barefoot, like all the children's. Suddenly she felt self-conscious in her own expensive clothes and shoes.

"That other boy, the fair-haired one, is mine. John. He's fifteen. And that there is Creed Allen, Rob's little brother," Mrs. Spencer said. She pointed to the red-haired boy who'd run into the cabin to announce that his father was hurt. "A rascal, that one is."

At the sound of his name, Creed looked up.

"This here's the new teacher from Asheville," Mrs. Spencer told him.

Rob and Creed stared at Christy. She couldn't read their faces. Was it curiosity or anger she saw there? Were they thinking that she was . . . that she was the cause of their father's accident?

Rob nodded shyly. "Proud to know you," he said softly. "I been lookin' forward to your comin' . . ." He turned back to his father, his voice trailing off.

His little brother ran over to eye Christy more closely. Overalls, tousled hair, lots of freckles—he looked like a character out of the book *Tom Sawyer*. His two front teeth were missing.

"Howdy-do," he said, head tilted to one side.

"I'm so sorry about your father," Christy said.

"It ain't your fault," the boy said. "Near as we can figure, Pa was cuttin' across Pebble Mountain when a high wind come up. A big tulip poplar tree bumped him right on the head."

"How'd you find him, Creed?" Mrs. Spencer asked, running her hand over his tangled hair.

"Me and Rob and John was huntin' squirrels out thataway. Bait-em—" He turned to Christy. "That's our old hound dog. Well, he nosed Pa right out. Tree was still on him."

Within minutes, a crowd began to form in the tiny Spencer cabin. Apparently word traveled fast out there in the mountains, even without telephones. Most of the people gathered seemed to be relatives of Mr. Allen.

The cabin was nearly full when Christy heard the stomping of feet and the whinny of a horse. A big-boned man strode inside, and the crowd parted. He had a shock of reddish, messy hair—hair that looked as if it had not seen a barber in a very long time. His features were rugged. Deep lines etched his face—or maybe it was just the long shadows cast by the kerosene lamp.

"That be Doc," Mrs. Spencer said.

"I'll be needing more light over here," the doctor said to Mrs. Spencer. His eyes fell on Christy. He stared at her for a moment, an intense gaze that seemed to go right through her, and for some reason Christy felt a blush flare in her cheeks.

"Neil MacNeill," he said in a deep voice.

"Christy Huddleston. I'm the new—"

Before she could finish, Dr. MacNeill had turned his back

on her. Mrs. Spencer brought another lamp close so he could begin his examination. He took off his coat and rolled up his shirt sleeves. The figure lying on the old post-and-spindle bed had not moved.

Mr. Pentland made his way through the crowd to Christy's side. "Doc MacNeill's the only doctor in the Cove," he explained.

Christy nodded and smiled up at him. She wished she could let him know how glad she was to have a friend in this awful situation, but an eerie silence had fallen on the room. All eyes were watching the doctor. The lamp cast giant shadows, dancing like monsters ready to spring from the walls. Only the draft of cold air seeping through a crack at Christy's back told her that this was all actually happening.

The doctor slid his fingers over Mr. Allen's head, feeling and probing. He took the patient's pulse, checked reflexes, opened the eyelids and stared intently into the eyes.

Finally he spoke, his face grim. "Bob's bad off," he said to a woman near the bed.

"Who's that?" Christy whispered to Mr. Pentland.

"That's Mary Allen, Bob's wife," the mailman answered. "And the man with the beard next to her is his brother Ault."

The woman's face was rigid with fear. "Is he goin' to die, Doc?"

The doctor's voice was gentle. "Don't know the answer to that, Mary. He's in a coma now, like a deep sleep. There's some bleeding inside his skull. If I leave the bleeding there, Bob will die."

He paused, looking around the room, as if lost in his own thoughts. For a moment, his eyes met Christy's. She thought she saw the glint of tears in them.

He probably blames me too, Christy thought. She felt like an outsider, the cause of all this horror. If she could have left, if there were anywhere for her to go, she would have.

"There's one chance of saving Bob, though," the doctor continued. "I could bore a small hole in his head, to let the bad blood out and try to lift the pressure. Mary, I want to tell you the truth. I've never tried this operation. I saw it done once. But it's a risky procedure. It's up to you, Mary. Will you let me try it?"

"I say no," the bearded man who was Bob's brother exclaimed. "Life and death is in the hands of the Lord. We've no call to tamper with it."

"No, Ault, you're wrong," Mary said. Her voice was firm. "We can't let go so long as there's one livin' breath left in Bob. We've got six young'uns to feed. Will you try, Doc?"

The doctor seemed unsure for a moment. Christy could see his problem. There wasn't much chance for the injured man, with or without the operation. With a mountain cabin for an operating room, no nurses, and little light, what chance did he have? Still, if Bob Allen died during the operation, it was likely that some of these mountain people would blame the doctor.

"All right, then," Dr. MacNeill said at last. "We'll go ahead."

He's made a courageous decision, Christy thought. Had there ever been such an awful setting for an operation? A baby crying, the smell of chewing tobacco, a crowd of people, dirty pots and pans by the hearth. It was hardly sanitary.

"We'll use the kitchen table," the doctor said. "Fairlight, I'll need boiling water and a hammer and awl. And somebody get me a couple of sawhorses and two or three boards. That will have to do for an instrument table. Those of you who aren't helping, stay out of the way, clear to one side. And no wailing or crying."

Soon the doctor's instruments were sterile and he was prepared to operate. As some of the men lifted Bob Allen onto the makeshift operating table, Christy heard a scuffle at the door. Suddenly Bob's wife dashed through the cabin. In her raised hands she held a razor-sharp ax. She lifted the ax high over her head and gave a mighty heave. Christy clapped her hand over her mouth to stifle a scream.

With a crash, the ax bit deep into the floorboard under the table.

Christy stared at the ax in stunned disbelief. But the doctor continued his work, unconcerned. Then Mary took a string and tied it around one of her husband's wrists.

"All right, Mary," said the doctor. "That's fine. That should be helpful. Will some of you take care of Mary until this is over?"

Mrs. Spencer led Mrs. Allen to a chair in a corner. "What was she doing with that ax?" Christy demanded of Mr. Pentland. "And the string . . . Is she crazy?"

"It's to protect Bob during the operation," Mr. Pentland explained matter-of-factly, as if surprised that Christy didn't understand. "The ax is to keep him from bleedin'. And the string is to keep disease away."

Once again Christy felt as if she'd entered a world where she didn't belong. Here people still believed in omens and witchcraft. It was as if these people had been born a century earlier.

"I'll need some help here," the doctor said, but no one moved forward in response.

He glanced over his shoulder. "You—do you have any nursing training?"

There was no answer. Christy realized he was speaking to her.

"Me? I—no," she stammered. "I'm a teacher."

"That'll do just fine. Come here."

Once again, as she had been at the station and this morning at the general store, Christy was aware of many eyes on her. She joined the doctor at the table. He was sharpening a razor on a strip of leather.

"You've got a strong stomach?" he asked.

"I—I don't know. I suppose so," Christy said.

The doctor gazed at her steadily, and for a moment she thought she saw a hint of a smile. "We'll know soon enough, I expect," he said. "I'm going to shave Bob's head. I just need you to hold it steady."

Carefully the doctor washed his hands in a basin. As he began shaving Mr. Allen's head, Christy tried her best to hold it steady while keeping her hands out of the way. Already, watching the smooth skin of the man's skull appear, she felt woozy. She wondered how long she would last in her new occupation as nurse. She felt herself swaying. To steady herself, she looked up at the ceiling.

"You still with me?" the doctor asked as he reached for his scalpel.

Christy swallowed. Her stomach did a somersault. "I'm fine," she lied.

"Good. Now, I'm going to be making my incision. Then I'll carefully drill the hole through Bob's skull. You may not want to watch."

"You may be right," Christy said, managing a weak smile.

"Bet you weren't expecting this when you set out for Cutter Gap," the doctor said.

"I'm starting to get used to the unexpected," Christy said.

"That'll serve you well here."

Christy glanced down at the thin red line trailing his scalpel. Quickly she looked away. She met the gaze of Mrs. Spencer, who was holding Mrs. Allen's hand. Mrs. Allen rocked back and forth, her face taut with fear.

"Steady now," said the doctor. "Keep a tight hold. Your legs holding out?"

"It's my stomach I'm worried about."

"Don't think about it," the doctor advised. "So you walked all the way here?"

Out of the corner of her eye, Christy could see the doctor setting down his scalpel and reaching for a thin, pointed metal tool. "With Mr. Pentland," she answered.

"In those frocks," Dr. MacNeill said, "I'm surprised you made it this far."

"So am I, now."

The doctor laughed slightly, then fell silent. "No movement," he commanded, his voice tense.

The room went still. Christy held Mr. Allen's head, his skin oddly cool against hers. Dr. MacNeill's breath was labored. A baby cried, then stopped, as if it understood the importance of the moment.

Christy tried not to think about what was happening just inches from her own hands. A man's skull was being opened. His life hung in the balance. Here, in this primitive cabin in the middle of nowhere, she was helping a doctor try to save a man's life.

If he died, it would be her fault.

There was only one thing to do now.

Christy closed her eyes and began to pray.

Six

"That's all, Miss Huddleston."

Christy looked up at the doctor in surprise. How long had he been working on Mr. Allen? How long had she been praying?

"I can finish up here," Dr. MacNeill said. "You get yourself some fresh air. I suspect you could use it."

Slowly Christy released her hold on Mr. Allen. "You're sure?"

"Quite sure. And thank you. You did a fine job."

Christy allowed herself a momentary glance at the patient. Mr. Allen's face was a ghastly white in the glow of the kerosene lamp. She caught sight of the incision the doctor had made, and her stomach climbed into her throat. She reached for the wall.

"I'll be . . . going, then," she said, making her way dizzily through the crowd.

Outside she breathed deeply of the cold air, trying to shake off the effect of the nightmarish scene. She shivered with the realization of what she'd just done. Was it only yesterday morning that she'd hugged her mother goodbye? How she longed for just a moment in the Huddlestons' warm parlor with its shiny piano and cozy, welcoming furniture. She'd never appreciated the cleanliness and beauty of it all. Not until now. . . .

She sat down on the porch steps. Around the yard, people milled in small groups. From time to time they would glance at her curiously, but no one approached. Instead, a small crowd had gathered around Mr. Spencer, who leaned against a tall pine, singing a song while he strummed a goose quill back and forth across the strings of a boxlike instrument. It had four strings and was shaped different from a guitar, with a slender waist and heart-shaped holes.

The simple melody seemed to wing its way into her mind and heart.

> *Down in the valley,*
>   *valley so low*
> *Hang your head over,*
>   *hear the wind blow.*
> *Hear the wind blow, love,*
>   *hear the wind blow;*
> *Hang your head over,*
>   *hear the wind blow.*

"You feelin' poorly, Miz Huddleston?" came a low voice. "You look a little pale."

Christy looked up to see Fairlight Spencer. The woman's bare feet in the snow sent a shiver through her. But all Mrs. Spencer seemed concerned about was Christy.

"I'm fine, thanks," Christy said. "The fresh air is doing me good. But you . . . Aren't you cold?"

"Land sakes, no. This is pretty near springlike to me. Warmed up considerable since yesterday."

"Tell me, Mrs. Spencer. What is that instrument your husband is playing?"

"That's a dulcimer," she replied. "Jeb, he loves to play."

They fell silent. Christy stared up at the tall peak nearly blotting out the winter sun. "It's beautiful here," she whispered. "I feel . . . like I'm in a whole different world."

Mrs. Spencer stared at her, as if she were trying to climb inside Christy for a moment and know what it was like. *She's only ten or so years older than I am*, Christy realized, despite all the children and the lines of worry near Fairlight's eyes.

Mrs. Spencer looked away, suddenly self-conscious. "Sorry," she apologized. "I guess I was just wonderin' what it would be like to come from your world. Is all your kin back in Asheville?"

Christy nodded. A sudden ache of homesickness fell over her like a shadow. She fingered the locket around her neck. "Would you like to see them?"

"I'd be right honored."

Christy took off the locket. Mrs. Spencer cupped it in her hand gently, as if she were holding a soap bubble.

"It opens—see?" Christy showed her how to unlock the silver heart.

Mrs. Spencer studied the pictures inside. "A mighty fine-looking family," she said. "Would that be you? There, lookin' all serious-like?"

Christy laughed. "That was at the church retreat last summer, right after I decided to come here. I suppose I was feeling pretty sure of myself."

Silence again fell between them. Gently, Mrs. Spencer returned the necklace to Christy.

"Mrs. Spencer," Christy said, "I think Fairlight is such a lovely name."

The mountain woman looked pleased. "I'd be right honored if you called me by my front name."

"Good. And you can call me Christy."

A few feet away, some of the children began a wild snowball fight. "You'll have your hands full over at the mission school, I expect," Fairlight said. "The Cove is full of youngsters." She grinned. "Mind you, some of 'em is more trouble than others."

"I'm sure I can handle them," Christy said. Even to her own ears, she didn't sound entirely convincing.

"I'm sure you can." Fairlight paused, staring up at the mountain peak bathed in shadow. "Still and all, if you ever . . ." She shook her head gently.

"What?"

"Nothin'. It was a crazy thought."

"Tell me," Christy urged. "Believe me, I've had my share of those."

Fairlight shrugged. "I was just goin' to say that if you ever need an extra pair of hands over to the school, I'd be mighty proud to help. That's a heap of young'uns for one gal. Maybe I could clean up the school after class?"

The words were spoken with a gentle dignity, as if a gift were being bestowed on Christy. Here was a mountain woman with a husband and five children to care for, living in such poverty that if she had any shoes, she was saving them to be worn somewhere special. Yet she was offering to help Christy, a girl she'd just met.

Even as Christy started to answer, she realized something else. This woman was not just volunteering to do some cleaning for her—she was also holding out the gift of her friendship. For the first time since leaving home, Christy sensed the possibility of connecting with people here, of not feeling quite so completely alone.

"Fairlight, that's a very kind offer," Christy said. "And I'll accept it—on one condition. I'm a long way from home, you know, and it would be nice to feel like I had a new friend here in the mountains. And maybe there'll be something I can do for you too."

The pioneer face was suddenly all smiles. "That you could, Miz Christy," she exclaimed. Suddenly she turned shy again, her voice sinking almost to a whisper. "I can't read nor write. Would . . . would you learn me how? I'd like that."

Her voice was filled with such eagerness that at that moment Christy wanted to teach this woman to read more than anything she'd ever wanted to do before.

"I'd love to do that, Fairlight. As soon as I get settled in at the mission. It's a promise."

"For sure and certain, that's wonderful to hear," Fairlight sighed, her face full of hope. And immediately Christy felt encouraged about her decision to come to Cutter Gap.

⌐#⌐

A few minutes later, a voice spoke from the shadows. "You must be real tired," Mr. Pentland said kindly. "Why don't I take you on out to the mission? It's not far now."

"But what about Mr. Allen? How is he? Is he . . ."

"Still livin' and breathin'," Mr. Pentland said. "Doc says he found the blood clots all right and Bob has a fightin' chance now. If the bleedin' in his head don't start up again."

"Oh, I'm glad. So glad," Christy said with relief.

Mr. Pentland reached for her suitcase. "Before you go, Doc said he wanted to see you."

"Me?" she asked.

She stepped back into the dark cabin. The doctor was sitting by Bob Allen's side, studying him seriously. He didn't even notice Christy until she spoke. "Doctor? You wanted to see me?"

He looked up wearily, rubbed his eyes, then gave a smile. "There she is. The Cove's answer to Florence Nightingale. I wanted to thank you for your help."

"I didn't do much," Christy said, gazing at the motionless patient. "And to tell you the truth, my knees nearly gave out there at the end. I couldn't wait to get outside."

He laughed, a deep, warm sound that filled the small cabin. "You should have seen me during my first surgery. Couldn't eat for two days afterward. And in any case, I knew you'd be fine."

"You did? How could you? I didn't even know."

He shrugged, then ran a hand through his messy curls. "The kind of girl who walks to the Cove in the middle of a January snowstorm has more courage than many." He looked her up and down. "You'll be needing it too."

She frowned. "Why does everyone keep warning me like that?"

"You'll see, soon enough," the doctor said. He grinned. "For starters, you'll have some characters there at the mission to deal with."

"Characters? You mean some of the children I'll be teaching?"

"Actually, I was referring to the adults there." He chuckled. "There's David Grantland, the new minister. His sister, Ida, is as crotchety as they come. And then there's Miss Alice, of course." He shook his head. "Now that's one interesting woman. Tough as can be."

"You didn't say anything about Mr. Grantland," Christy pointed out.

"Didn't I?" the doctor said, a glimmer in his eye. "David's a good man. Just new to these parts and still learning. He's more than a little stubborn. In any case, I have a hunch you'll manage just fine."

"I hope you're right." She touched Bob Allen's fingers with her own. "He'll be all right?"

"He's not out of the woods yet. The next few hours will tell the tale."

"I feel . . . so responsible. It's my fault he's here."

"Nonsense," the doctor said. "Don't you go worrying about things like that. You'll have plenty to keep you busy without taking responsibility for falling trees."

Christy turned to leave, then paused at the door. "Will I see you again?" She saw his smile and quickly changed her words. "I mean, how will I know if Mr. Allen is all right?"

"Oh, you'll hear soon enough," said Dr. MacNeill. "Word travels fast."

She was halfway out the door when he added, "And yes."
"Yes?"

"Yes, we'll see each other again. I've no doubt of that." He gave a fleeting smile, then turned all his attention back to his patient.

Christy found Mr. Pentland waiting outside. She said goodbye to the Spencers, then fell into step behind the mailman. She'd had all the walking she wanted for one day—for one month, come to think of it—but she had no choice but to follow him and hope that when he said "not far" he really meant it.

As they headed from the cabin, she could hear Mr. Spencer begin to sing again. It was such a sad melody, the kind of song that seemed to belong here in this lonely and forbidding place.

They walked in silence. It was just as well, since Christy was far too tired for conversation. Questions swirled around in her head like the snowflakes blown loose from the tall trees swaying overhead.

She didn't believe in omens. She wasn't the least bit superstitious (although she had been known to avoid walking under ladders). But she couldn't help wondering if Mr. Allen's accident was some sort of signpost, telling her she had made a mistake, pointing her back to the world where she belonged.

"Not much farther now," Mr. Pentland called back to her. "We've just got the bridge to cross, and then the mission is right over the next ridge."

"Bridge?" Christy asked. Her throat tightened as she remembered waking up from her terrible dream that morning at Mrs. Tatum's. Had it just been this morning?

She quickened her pace. "This bridge . . . Is it a big one?" she asked, trying to sound casual.

Mr. Pentland considered. "Not too big. Big enough, I s'pose. Gets real slippery-like when it ices up." He glanced at Christy's face. "Don't worry none, though."

They trudged along the snowy trail for two hundred more

yards until the sound of rushing water met Christy's ears. Around a bend, the swirling waters of a half-frozen stream came into view. A creek, Mr. Pentland had called it, but it moved, even choked with ice, with the speed of a raging river.

Her gaze moved upward. Then she saw it.

"Th—that's the bridge?"

"Yep."

But it was not a bridge at all, just two huge, uneven logs with a few thin boards nailed across here and there. A deadly layer of ice coated all of it.

Christy joined Mr. Pentland near the edge of the bridge. The whole contraption swayed in the biting wind.

"I'll go first to see if it's too slippery," Mr. Pentland said. He shifted the mail pouch to the middle of his back and regripped Christy's suitcase, then paused, scraping his feet on the edge of the bridge.

Christy kept her eyes on his feet as he stepped onto the wood. Halfway across he stopped. Below him, the water sprayed over the boulders in the middle of the creek. "Ain't so bad," he called back. "Wait until I get across, though, so you won't get no sway."

Carefully he finished crossing. "Stomp your feet now," he called from the other side. "Get 'em warm. Then come on—but first scrape your boots, then hike up your skirts."

As frozen and unmoving as the landscape around her, Christy stood staring at the bridge. The sound of the water became a roar in her ears. There was no turning back now. Slowly, very slowly, she began to make her way across the log bridge.

Then it was her worst nightmare, come true. She was slipping . . . screaming . . . falling toward the icy water below.

Seven

Cold. The water was so cold. Instantly thoughts of the last two days swept away behind her, and Christy was left struggling to breathe. She opened her mouth, but there was only icy water where air should be. She felt it rush inside her, into her throat, into her lungs. She grabbed for the surface with all her being, but something kept pulling her down.

She was choking. She was dying, and all she wanted was air—one sweet, clean breath of air. The water in her lungs should have been cold, but it burned like she'd breathed in fire. She stroked with all her might against the current, frantically trying to propel herself toward the surface. Her hand broke through to air, and she groped for it as if she could breathe with her fingers, as if her fingers could suck in the precious oxygen she wanted so badly.

God, don't let me die here, she prayed desperately. *Not yet . . . there's still so much I want to do, Lord.*

She thought of her family, of their horror upon learning that their daughter had died this way, in a mountain creek far from home, far from love. She thought of the school where she'd wanted to change lives. She was doing something that would really make a difference. She had to make it.

The current sucked her down again, but this time she groped at the frigid water with renewed fury. Her hand broke through once more, and again she felt the air. But this time someone grabbed her hand.

As if in slow, slow motion, she was pulled from the icy grip of the current. At last, she could breathe.

⌁

Someone wrapped a blanket around her. She tried to talk, but she was coughing too hard. Violent shivers shook her whole body, as if someone were shaking her and wouldn't let go.

Strong arms lifted her into the air. Someone was carrying her. Christy blinked, tried to focus. It wasn't Mr. Pentland. Who was this man?

"Feel like anything's broken?" the man asked.

Christy shook her head.

"She's a feisty one, that gal," came Mr. Pentland's familiar voice. "Reckon she'll be fine."

They began to walk, and Christy realized that this man, whoever he was, was going to carry her the rest of the way to the mission. "Good thing she's not any heavier," he said to Mr. Pentland.

She heard the humor in his voice and started to answer, but all that came out was a raw, hacking cough.

"I'm David Grantland, by the way."

"Chr—" Christy paused to cough. "Christy Hud—"

"Huddleston. Yes, I know. We've been expecting you. You really know how to make an entrance, I must say."

Christy gazed up at his handsome face. Mr. Grantland had black hair, fine white teeth, and friendly brown eyes set wide apart. And there was something about his nose—it looked a little different, as if it might have had a run-in with a baseball or a fist somewhere along the way.

"I'm sorry," Christy managed to say. "I guess I slipped—"

"You were lucky," Mr. Grantland said. "You could've hit one of those rocks."

"Lucky you came along when you did," Mr. Pentland said. "By the time I'd have gotten down to the bank, no telling where she mighta been."

"I was on my way to the bunkhouse just up the hill when I saw you two coming," Mr. Grantland explained.

"We stopped over to the Spencers' on the way," Mr. Pentland said. "Wait'll ya hear what happened to ol' Bob Allen."

While Mr. Pentland recounted the story of Mr. Allen's surgery, Christy rested her cheek against Mr. Grantland's shoulder. She felt a little embarrassed, being carried this way like a helpless child, but she was too wet and exhausted and cold and battered to much care. The steady rock of Mr. Grantland's steps and the lull of his deep voice pulled her closer and closer to sleep.

She had just shut her eyes when Mr. Pentland said, "Here we go. Told ya it weren't too far."

Christy lifted her head. Ahead of them stood the mission house—a large square framed building set in a big yard with a mountain rising behind it.

"There it is," Mr. Grantland said. "Home sweet home."

The front door of the mission house opened to reveal an older woman. She was tall, almost gaunt, with angular features. "What in the world has the cat dragged in?" she demanded.

"Miss Huddleston fell into the creek," Mr. Grantland said. He stepped inside the house. The warmth on her icy face brought tears to Christy's eyes.

"Think you can stand?" he asked.

Christy nodded.

"Good thing," he said. "Nothing personal, but my arms are about to give out."

He set her down gently. Instantly the room began to sway, and he held out an arm to steady her. He pointed to the older woman.

"This is my sister, Ida. Her bark, you'll soon find, is worse than her bite."

"You may call me Miss Ida." The woman clucked her tongue at the puddle forming on the floor. "Look at this mess! She brought half the creek in with her."

"Now, Ida," Mr. Grantland chided. "Miss Huddleston has had a rough day."

"That she has," Mr. Pentland agreed. "Walked all the way here, she did. Then helped the doc with his surgery, and plumb fell off a bridge to boot."

Miss Ida seemed to soften a little. "Let's get you upstairs and into some dry clothes," she said, leading Christy toward the stairway.

Christy turned. She gave a weak smile to Mr. Pentland and Mr. Grantland. "Thank you," she said. "Thank you both for everything."

Mr. Pentland gave a courtly nod. Mr. Grantland grinned. "Not at all," he said. "It isn't every day I get to save a damsel in distress."

His sister rolled her eyes. "Damsel in distress, indeed!"

She took Christy's suitcase and helped her up the wooden stairs, all the while grimacing at the trail of muddy water Christy was leaving in her wake. At the top of the stairs, Miss Ida gestured to a simple room. It was not luxurious, to say the least—a washstand with a white china pitcher and bowl, an old dresser with a cracked mirror above it, two straight chairs, the plainest kind of white curtains, and two cotton rag rugs on the bare floor.

"First things first," Miss Ida said. "We need to get you into some dry clothes." She handed Christy some towels.

"I have some things . . ." Christy paused ". . . in my suitcase." She was tired, so tired. Had she ever been this exhausted? The very insides of her bones ached. Never had a bed looked so inviting.

Miss Ida unlatched the suitcase. She pulled out Christy's diary and set it aside. Carefully she removed a nightgown. "Here, now," she said. "You get yourself good and dry, then put on this nightgown. Whatever you do, don't sit on that bed in those soaking clothes."

Too tired to respond, Christy did as she was told. By the time Miss Ida returned, Christy had managed to put on her nightgown and run a comb through her tangled, wet hair. Miss Ida frowned at the pile of wet clothes in the corner.

"I'll take care of those tomorrow," Christy promised, feeling guilty at the awful impression she must be making. She glanced longingly at the bed—the soft, warm, and very dry bed.

With a grimace, Miss Ida picked up the wet clothes. "I'll take care of them," she said in a long-suffering tone.

"Thank you, Miss Ida. I'm so sorry to be such trouble. I

guess I'm not making a very good impression . . ." Christy's voice faded off.

"Oh, you seemed to have made quite an impression on my brother," Miss Ida said flatly.

Christy attempted a smile, but Miss Ida did not return it. "I suppose you'll be wanting something to eat?" Miss Ida asked.

"The truth is I'm too tired to eat."

"Well, then. You can get yourself settled in tomorrow. Miss Alice will be wanting to meet you."

"I'm looking forward to it. And I can't wait to see the school."

For a moment, Miss Ida's expression warmed. "The building's almost complete. David did most of it himself. It's a sight to behold."

"I hope I do it justice," Christy said.

"I do too," Miss Ida replied. The tone in her voice told Christy that she had her doubts.

At last the door closed and Christy was alone in her little room. Her whole body ached. She could tell she was going to have a nasty bruise on her hip from her fall.

She retrieved her diary and pen. She wanted to keep track of her adventure as it unfolded, and so much had happened today. As exhausted as she was, she had to get it all down while it was still fresh in her mind.

She climbed into bed. The clean sheets felt wonderful as she propped herself up against her pillow with the diary on her knees.

"Where should I begin?" she wrote.

A few words, that's all. Just a few words . . .

Slowly her eyelids began to droop. Tired. She was so very

tired . . . She set down her pen and lay her head against the pillow, her eyes already closing. As she pulled the sheets up to her chin, her hand grazed her neck. It was only then she realized her locket was gone. It had come off, no doubt, during her tumble into the creek.

I'll go back, she told herself. *Maybe, by some miracle, I'll find it.*

But as she fell into a deep, dreamless sleep, in her heart she knew the truth: that the locket had been lost in the raging mountain creek. But she also knew that she must not dwell on the loss of her precious family keepsake. Instead, she must put her old life behind her and concentrate on beginning a new life in this strange place.

Eight

CHRISTY SLEPT LATE THE NEXT MORNING. WHEN SHE awoke, her body was stiff and sore. Just as she'd expected, there was a large, ugly bruise on her hip.

The events of the previous day seemed like a dream. But if they were all a dream, what was she doing in this strange little room? The long and exhausting walk, the Spencers' cabin, Mr. Allen's surgery, her terrifying fall off the bridge . . . Had it all happened in the space of one short day?

Christy reached for the place at her throat where her locket should have been. She couldn't believe she'd lost it. What would she tell her father?

She hobbled stiffly over to one of the windows. Nothing had prepared her for what met her eyes. Mountain ranges were folded one behind the other. Some were snow covered. Others showed patches of emerald or deep green. And then the blues began. On the smoky blue of the far summits, fluffy white clouds rested like wisps of cotton.

She counted the mountain ranges. Eleven of them, rising up and up toward the vault of the sky.

Only yesterday at the Spencer cabin, watching a man undergo surgery because of her, Christy had wondered if accepting this teaching job had been a dreadful mistake. Now, staring at this peaceful view, she was not quite so sure what to think. Had Mr. Allen survived the night? She still did not know. But meanwhile, in the face of tragedy, these mountains were whispering a different message to her. A message that seemed to say, *Stay. This is your view. This will be your source of peace and strength.*

Someone knocked on her door. It was Miss Ida. For the first time, Christy got a good look at her. She was a plain woman with thin, graying hair. It was drawn into a tight bun, so meager that her scalp showed through in several places. Her nose was too large for her narrow face. Already Christy could tell she was a nervous person. When she smiled, it seemed to be an afterthought, as if her brain had ordered, "Now, smile," but her feelings hadn't joined in.

"You slept well, I hope?" Miss Ida asked.

"Just fine."

"I've cleaned up your clothes. They're downstairs, drying."

"Thank you so much," Christy said gratefully. "Oh, Miss Ida, tell me—I've got to know. Mr. Allen, how is he? Is he . . ." She couldn't quite say it.

"Alive? Oh, yes. Dr. MacNeill spent the night there. Miss Alice Henderson too. She went right to the Spencers' soon as she heard about the operation. She's catching a wink of sleep now."

"Then Mr. Allen's out of danger?"

"Not yet, I take it, or the doctor wouldn't still be there. Now about breakfast—everybody else has eaten. When you get changed, come on down to the dining room. I'll see you get something."

Christy wondered who "everybody" was. How many lived in this house?

"Miss Alice would like to see you today," Miss Ida said. She crossed the room to the window and pointed. "See that smoke? That's her cabin. Just there, beyond the trees."

After Miss Ida left, Christy dressed quickly and rushed downstairs. She felt as if she hadn't eaten in days. The dining room turned out to be a simple square room at the back of the house. A round, golden-oak table sat in the center.

Miss Ida provided a wonderful breakfast: hot oatmeal followed by buckwheat cakes and maple syrup. "David's at the Low Gap School near here," Miss Ida said as she watched Christy eat. "He said to tell you he was sorry not to be here when you woke up."

"I'm sorry I overslept. Does Mr. Grantland teach at that school?"

"Oh, no, that school is closed. There were some old school desks there. They said we could use them. Supplies, you'll soon see, are always a problem here." She pointed out the window to an unfinished building about a thousand yards away. It was rectangular, with a half-finished bell tower. "David can build anything he sets his hand to," she said proudly. "He's working on the steeple now."

"Then will that be the church as well as the school?"

"That's right," Miss Ida said, with a tone in her voice that made Christy uncomfortable. "We haven't the lumber and funds here to put up two buildings when one would do. This will be used for school on weekdays and church on Sundays."

"They've never had a school here before?"

Miss Ida watched, curling her lip just slightly, as Christy helped herself to a second round of buckwheat cakes. "You've quite an appetite, haven't you?" she asked. "But you asked about the school. No, this will be the first term."

"Does Mr. Grantland live here, in the mission house?"

Miss Ida shook her head. "He has a bunkhouse down by the creek. That's why it's lucky you fell in there. He and Miss Alice take their meals here in the house, though." She smiled proudly. "David begged me to come and keep house for him. He says maybe we can find a mountain woman to train as a housekeeper. But I have doubts myself that anybody else can cook to suit him."

Just then the side door banged, and suddenly Mr. Grantland stood in the kitchen doorway. A young girl with snarled red hair peered curiously from behind him. "Miss Huddleston," he said with a smile, "I must say you're looking much better—not to mention drier—this morning."

"I'm not sure I thanked you properly yesterday," Christy said.

"For . . . ?"

"For everything. For carrying me here, for . . ." She hesitated as the words sank in. "For saving my life."

Mr. Grantland laughed. His big, booming voice filled the room. "All in a day's work. Oh—" He turned and beckoned to the red-haired girl. "Allow me to introduce Ruby Mae Morrison. She's staying here at the mission house with us for a while."

The girl stepped forward. "Howdy," she said eagerly. Her eyes took in every inch of Christy. She was a teenager, maybe thirteen or so, Christy guessed, with abundant red hair that looked as if it had not been combed in a long while. Her plain, thin cotton dress was torn at the hem. She was barefoot, just as the Spencer children had been.

"Nice to meet you, Ruby Mae," Christy said. She pointed to some leftover buckwheat cakes. "Would you two like to join me?"

"They both had breakfast," Miss Ida reminded Christy primly. "Hours ago."

"Reckon I'm hungry again, though," Ruby Mae said, pulling up a chair.

Miss Ida sighed. "I suppose, if Miss Huddleston is done, you may as well finish up what's left. But, please, Ruby Mae, go wash up in the basin in the kitchen."

"Wash up, wash up, wash up," Ruby Mae muttered, rolling her eyes heavenward as she reluctantly headed for the kitchen. "If'n I wash up much more, I'll wash my skin clean off!"

Mr. Grantland laughed as she disappeared into the kitchen. "She's a character, that one," he said.

"She's trouble, is what he means," Miss Ida said, scraping crumbs from the table into her palm. "She'll talk your ear off if you let her. And gossip! Where that girl gets her information, I'll never know."

"Ruby Mae is a one-woman newspaper," Mr. Grantland said.

"Why—" Christy lowered her voice— "why is she staying here?"

His face went serious. "She and her stepfather don't get along. After a particularly bad argument, he ordered her out of the cabin. She had nowhere else to go, so we took her in."

Ruby Mae returned, thrusting her hands in front of Miss Ida for inspection. "Ain't no more of those germy things a-growin' on these hands," she declared. She winked at Christy. "Not that I've ever seen one, mind you. But Doc MacNeill and Miss Ida and Miss Alice, they keep a-swearin' they're there." She pointed to Christy's plate. "You done with those?"

"Oh—yes. Here, please. I couldn't eat another bite." Christy passed her plate to Ruby Mae, who began to eat like she hadn't seen food in weeks.

"She's got the appetite of a grown man, that girl," Miss Ida said with evident distaste.

"That's all right," Christy said, smiling at Ruby Mae. "So do I."

Ruby Mae grinned back gratefully, her mouth stuffed with buckwheat cakes. "Maybuf latef I shoof yoouf aroumf."

"Allow me to translate," Mr. Grantland said. "I speak Ruby Mae. I believe she was offering to give you the royal tour of the mission."

Ruby Mae nodded enthusiastically.

"Which would probably be a fine idea," he continued, "since I, unfortunately, cannot do the honors myself. I've got another load of school desks to pick up."

"I'd like that, Ruby Mae," Christy said.

Ruby Mae glowed, obviously thrilled at being assigned such an important duty.

"I'm afraid it will be a rather brief tour," Mr. Grantland said. "There's not much to see, really."

"Oh, yes, there is," Christy replied. "When I looked out my window this morning, it practically took my breath away. The mountains, the sky . . . It's amazing."

"Yes," Mr. Grantland gazed at her thoughtfully. "I'm glad you can see that too." His voice went soft. "Sometimes, with all the problems here in the Cove, it helps to see God's beauty in His creation." He smiled a little self-consciously. "Well, I must be off. Enjoy your tour. And enjoy your meeting with Miss Alice."

He gave a little wave and in a few long strides had disappeared out the door.

Ruby Mae leaned across the table. Her mouth was still full of buckwheat cakes.

"Swallow," Miss Ida chided.

Ruby Mae obeyed dutifully, but not without another roll of her lively brown eyes. "He's not married, you know," she confided to Christy in a loud whisper.

"You mean . . . Mr. Grantland?" Christy asked uncomfortably, noting Miss Ida's grimace.

"He don't even have a gal-friend, near as I can tell. And believe you me, I would know. I keep up on everybody's comings and goings."

"David has his mind on far more important things than a gal-friend, Ruby Mae," Miss Ida snapped. "He's here to do the work of the Lord, not to fall in love."

"I reckon sometimes that's sort of the same thing, ain't it?" Ruby Mae asked thoughtfully.

Christy tried very hard to hide her smile. It was clear that Miss Ida was not amused.

⌒#⌐

"And this here's the outhouse," Ruby Mae said with a grin. "Reckon you ain't seen nothing this fancy before."

Christy blinked. Actually, the outdoor toilet was more primitive than anything she'd ever seen. And drafty, too, in this January cold.

It had not occurred to her how simple the mission buildings would be. She gazed back at the white three-story framed building with a screened porch on either side. The mission house where she'd slept last night was a palace compared to the Spencer cabin, of course. But still, there was no electricity, no telephone, no plumbing. The house, along with the church-schoolhouse, a lattice-covered springhouse, the double outhouse, Mr. Grantland's bunkhouse by the creek, and Miss Henderson's cabin, were the only buildings at the mission.

"It's a fine outhouse," Christy managed to say, and Ruby Mae beamed with pride, as if she'd built it herself.

The girl had not stopped talking during Christy's tour of the mission. One question, one smile from Christy, was all it took for Ruby Mae to break into a beaming grin so full of excitement that Christy wondered when the last time was that anyone had really paid attention to the girl. Would all her students be this needy, this dying for affection? As Ruby Mae's questions began to accumulate, so did Christy's. She was anxious to talk to Miss Alice and get some answers.

"And now, for the finest part of my showin'," Ruby Mae announced. "The school!" She took Christy's hand and led her toward the simple church building. "I saved the best for very last."

Christy followed Ruby Mae up the wooden steps. As they entered the building, the girl fell silent for the first time.

The school room smelled of varnish and woodsmoke. A small potbellied stove sat in one corner. A few battered school desks were scattered across the floor.

Slowly Christy walked to the teacher's desk near the stove.

This was hers. This was where she would soon be teaching. This was where her adventure really would begin.

"Fills ya up with excitement, don't it, just to come inside?" Ruby Mae asked in a hushed voice.

It's the same voice you would use in a church, Christy thought. Then she realized this was a church every Sunday.

"I can't tell you how much we all have been lookin' forward to havin' a real school with a real live teacher," Ruby Mae said sincerely.

Christy smiled. "I hope I turn out to be a real live teacher."

"I don't rightly see your point," Ruby Mae said, her face puckered up in concentration.

"It's just—" Christy stared into the girl's bright eyes. "Well, I've never taught before, you see. I suppose I'm a little nervous."

"You, nervous? That's a good one!" Ruby Mae laughed loudly, slapping her leg, as if she'd never heard anything funnier. Slowly she realized Christy was serious. Her face went instantly solemn. "Oh, Miz Huddleston, I declare. I weren't laughing at you. It's just that I figure it's us students who have the right to be all nervous-like. I mean, Lordamercy, you're the teacher!"

I'm the teacher. Christy tried out the words in her mind. She liked the sound of them.

Sure, it had been a long and dangerous journey here. Sure, things hadn't gone as she'd hoped so far. But what was she so worried about? Ruby Mae was right. Christy was the teacher.

Now that she was finally here, what else could possibly go wrong?

Nine

THAT AFTERNOON, CHRISTY KNOCKED ON THE DOOR OF Miss Alice Henderson's cabin. She took a deep breath to calm herself. Already the stories about Miss Alice had impressed her. She wanted to do her very best to impress Miss Alice too.

The woman who answered the door had beautiful, clear features and deep gray eyes that looked both excited and tired at the same time. Her hair had once been blond, but now was sprinkled with gray. She was wearing a straight, blue woolen skirt and a clean, white linen blouse. Mr. Pentland had said there was something queenlike about her, and he was right.

"Do come in," she said, staring intently at Christy.

Stepping into Miss Henderson's cabin was almost like going home to Asheville. There was warmth and color and shine here. Firelight gleamed on the old pine and cherry furniture and the polished brass and pewter. Windows along the back of the room brought the beautiful Cutter Gap scenery indoors. The winter landscape and the towering peaks filled the room like a gigantic mural.

Christy had not realized how homesick she was until she

felt the relief pouring through her. There *was* some beauty and order here in the Cove! It wasn't all just plainness and poverty.

"Come, sit down, child," Miss Henderson urged. "Does my cabin surprise you?"

"I'm sorry. I didn't mean to stare. After that nightmare scene yesterday at the Spencers', I wasn't sure that I . . . that I belonged here. But this is so beautiful that I want to hug it—if you could hug a room. It's like . . . Well, like coming home."

"That's the nicest compliment my cabin's ever had. Here, sit by the fire. Got down to ten below zero this morning."

"Miss Henderson," Christy asked, almost afraid to hear the answer, "how is Mr. Allen?"

"About seven this morning he opened his eyes and asked about his ailing hound dog. I think he's going to be all right."

Christy felt relief wash over her like a warm breeze. Now she wouldn't have to live with the guilt of thinking she'd caused Mr. Allen's death.

Miss Henderson sat down across from Christy. "Now, tell me, Miss Huddleston," she said suddenly. "Why did you come to Cutter Gap?"

Surely she must be joking, Christy thought. But one look at her face told Christy she was not. "Naturally, I thought Dr. Ferrand would have told you," Christy answered. "I came to teach school, of course."

"He didn't tell me much. And anyway, I want to hear your version. Why are you here?"

It was such a complicated question. Christy hesitated. Where should she begin? "I was so moved at the church retreat when I heard about the mountain people," she began slowly. "I volunteered right away."

"Looking back," Miss Henderson asked, smoothing out a crease in her skirt, "do you think you were carried away by the emotion of the moment?"

"Somewhat, perhaps," Christy admitted. She wanted to be completely honest with this woman. Something about Miss Henderson demanded honesty.

"And Dr. Ferrand is eloquent," Miss Henderson pointed out.

"But I've had plenty of time to think it over," Christy added quickly. "If I'd wanted to back out, I could have."

"And why didn't you?"

"Because I knew you were desperate for teachers. I've had a year and a semester of college, enough to start teaching. And—" She paused. It was so hard to explain what was in her heart. "I'd like my life to count for something."

Miss Henderson fell silent. It was different from the embarrassing lapses in conversation Christy had felt, talking to a boy she liked or a person she didn't know. This was a silence full of meaning, a comfortable silence.

Christy longed to tell Miss Henderson about the feeling she'd had that there was some special mission waiting for her. Maybe that feeling just came from reading too much poetry—or because she was young. But Christy didn't think so. She wanted her life to be full. She wanted to laugh and love. She wanted to help others. Those were the hopes that had sent her on this wild adventure into the mountains.

But she couldn't explain those things, not yet. So she just sat silently, staring at her hands.

"You'll need some information about your new job," Miss Henderson said, suddenly changing the subject. "School opens on Monday next. Your coming gives us an official staff of three: David, you, and me, with Dr. Ferrand in overall charge. By the way, those at the mission call me 'Miss Alice.' David you've already met. He just graduated from the seminary. He's from Pennsylvania, like me."

"How long have you been here, Miss Alice?"

"I first came to the Great Smokies almost nine years ago. I started several schools in the area, then I saw Cutter Gap and loved it. I felt this was my spot." She gazed around the room. "I wanted this cabin to be a sort of sanctuary, a quiet spot for me and for other people, where they could talk out some of their problems when they want to."

"You mean the mountaineers?"

"They prefer to be called mountain people or highlanders. And believe me, there's plenty of problems for them to talk out. These people were brought up on a religion of fear. I believe one of our tasks here is to show folks a God who wants to give them joy. How they need joy!"

Her eyes took on a soft, remembering look. "I am a Quaker, you may know. My father was a strict member of the Society of Friends. But he had one favorite saying as I grew up. 'Before God,' he would say to me, 'I've just one duty as a father. That is to see that thee has a happy childhood tucked under thy jacket.'"

"I like that," Christy said, grinning at the image. "And did you have a happy childhood?"

"The happiest imaginable." Her voice trailed off. "I would like a little of that for these children. They have such hard lives."

"I'm afraid the hardness is all I've seen so far."

Miss Alice nodded with understanding. "At first I couldn't see anything but the dirt and the poverty either. But as I got to know the people better, flashes of something else began to come through. It's like looking through a peephole into the past. The old ballads, the words from another century. You'll see. These are tough people, proud and self-reliant, with an intense love of freedom. They've got iron wills that could bring major achievements." She sighed. "Of course, now their wills are used mainly to keep feuds alive."

Christy shifted uneasily, remembering the warnings of the train conductor and Mrs. Tatum. "You mean real shooting feuds?"

"Real shooting-and-killing feuds." For the first time, Miss Alice's face was grim.

"What do you and Mr. Grantland do about it?"

"Well, the first thing I did was buy a gun and learn to shoot."

Christy's mouth dropped open in surprise. "You did! But I thought the Quakers—"

"Believe in nonviolence. You're right. I've had my dear ancestors spinning in their graves ever since. Now that I've seen violence close up, I believe in nonviolence more than ever. But I had to meet these men on their own ground. So now I'm a better shot than a lot of them, and they all know it and respect it. I tell them, 'I like your fierce pride and your loyalty to your family. That's why I long to keep you from doing anything that will shame your sons and your sons' sons.'"

The room was very quiet as Christy considered the Quaker lady's words. *I can learn much from this woman,* Christy thought, *if only she will teach me.*

When at last Christy rose to go, Miss Alice held out her hand. "Christy Huddleston," she said, "I think you will do."

The warmth of her voice brought unexpected tears to Christy's eyes. She hoped Miss Alice was right.

⌒

That night, Christy sat in her bed, her diary propped on her knees. During dinner, she'd discussed lesson plans with Mr. Grantland and Miss Alice. They'd seemed a little amused at her ambitious ideas.

"Don't bite off more than you can chew," Mr. Grantland had warned. "We're talking about a lot of students, a lot of ages. You'll be lucky to get them all to sit still for an hour."

Christy chewed on the top of her pen, considering. At the top of a fresh page, she wrote:

GOALS FOR SCHOOL YEAR:

(1) Establish basic reading and arithmetic skills

(2) Penmanship exercises

(3) Calculus?

(4) French lessons?

(5) Latin?

(6) Music lessons?

(7) Hygiene and etiquette?

She scanned her list. Well, maybe etiquette was too much. It didn't much matter if you knew which fork to use if you didn't own any forks. Still, she had to set standards, didn't she? She had to aim high.

And what was the goal that Miss Alice had mentioned? *To show folks a God who wants to give them joy.* Now, that was a tall order. How could Christy begin to show these poor people what joy meant?

She thought about the question Miss Alice had asked her today. Again, she began to write:

Miss Alice asked me why I've come here to Cutter Gap. It's a good question. It made me think back to my life in Asheville, full of parties and pretty things. Of course, there was nothing wrong with that life—in fact, now I see how very blessed I have been. But I can't help wondering what it all meant. Where was it leading?

There must be more to life than that. Or is there—for a woman?

What was I born for, after all? I have to know. If I'd stayed at home, going the round of the same parties, I don't think I ever would have known. Mother and Father didn't understand why I was so anxious to come here. But I couldn't wait forever.

Come Monday, I won't have to wait any longer.

Ten

"You okay?" Mr. Grantland inquired on Monday morning. "You look a little green around the gills."

Christy gave him a weak smile. "Butterflies," she said.

"I'm not sure I follow."

"My stomach. It's full of butterflies. So full it's amazing I haven't fluttered away." She gazed at him hopefully. "Was it like this for you, the first time you preached a sermon, Mr. Grantland?"

"Don't you think it's time you started calling me David?" he asked.

"David," she amended.

"And the answer is yes. Matter of fact, I still get the shakes every Sunday. Feel better?"

"Not much."

He laughed then extended his arm. They started down the steps of the mission house.

For this first day of school, David had put away his working clothes and was dressed in a tweed suit with a white shirt and bow tie. He wore heavy boots, laced almost to his knees, because of the deep snow. The boots made Christy's dainty shoes, with their pointed toes and patent leather, look even sillier.

Carefully she picked her way across the cleaned boardwalk that led to the school.

"Is this a fashion parade on Fifth Avenue in New York?" David teased. "Those are silly, silly shoes. Ice-pick toes!"

"I know," Christy admitted. She'd wanted to look just right for her first day, but suddenly she saw herself through the eyes of the mountain children. She would look silly and overdressed to them. "Is it too late to change?"

"Yes," he said, shaking his head.

Her right shoe began to skid on the boardwalk. "Hold on!" David called, reaching out his arm to support her. "We don't want you slipping again!"

She could feel the warmth of his hand even through her coat. She wondered if her hair still looked all right and if he liked the way she'd worn it.

But suddenly she had more important things to worry about. The schoolyard was swarming with children waiting for the first glimpse of their new teacher. Their high-pitched voices rang in the clear air. Most were skinny, too pale, and none were dressed warmly enough for January.

Christy hesitated, watching them run in and out of the school building. So many students. And so lively! What if she couldn't handle them all?

"These children are really excited," David said. "You'd be surprised what a big event the opening of this school is in these people's lives."

As they noticed Christy and David approaching, the children stopped to stare.

A little boy detached himself from the group and came running up to Christy. He had carrot-red hair and blue eyes. "Teacher," he said with a shy eagerness, "I've come to see you and to swap howdies. I memorized your name. It shore is a funny name. I never heard a name like it afore."

"Miss Huddleston," David said solemnly, "this is Little Burl Allen, one of Bob Allen's sons."

So this was one of the children who would have been fatherless if Dr. MacNeill had not operated. All over again Christy felt grateful for the good news she'd heard about Mr. Allen.

She reached down for the little boy's hand. It was cold. "I'm delighted to swap howdies with you, Little Burl." He was so little—and those icy feet! She longed to pick him up and get him warm.

They headed up the steps to the school. As they entered, they were met by the smell of wet wool and cedar pencils. Already there were puddles of water on the floor from the melted snow the children had tracked in. Most of the children filed up to the teacher's desk to get a better look at Christy. Many of the girls were too shy to say anything, but the boys whispered furiously to each other. Christy overheard snatches:

"Got uncommon pretty eyes, ain't she?"

"You're already stuck on the teacher!"

"Reckon she'll have us a-studyin' like dogs?"

"Naw. She's too little to tan any britches!"

It took almost fifteen minutes before David could drag the children away from Christy's desk and quiet them down. To Christy's surprise, the girls seated themselves on one side of the room and the boys on the other.

"Why are they separated that way?" Christy whispered to David after he shooed a straggler to his seat.

"Tradition," he said. "That's how their people have done it for centuries. Same way at church on Sunday."

Christy stood beside the battered teacher's desk on its raised platform and surveyed her class. Several of the pupils actually seemed to be as old as she was—including the three boys who had been the last ones to slink into the schoolroom. She noticed David eyeing them warily and wondered if they might be troublemakers.

On the other hand, some of the children were tiny, not more than five years old. They wore a strange assortment of clothes—including coats several sizes too big with sleeves turned up. Many of the youngsters looked very tired, with the serious, worn faces of old men and women.

"Ladies and gentlemen," David began, sending the class into a chorus of giggles, "I am indeed honored today to introduce to you our new schoolteacher, Miss Huddleston."

While he spoke, Christy tried to count the number of children in the room. She counted the number of desks in each row—nine—and the number of rows—eight. Seventy-two, with five desks empty. It was unbelievable. How could one teacher handle sixty-seven squirming children? All at once her careful lesson plans seemed crazy. No wonder David and Miss Alice had warned her about being too ambitious.

The introduction was over. Christy moved to the front of the desk. "Thank you," she began. "I—I'm glad to be here. I know that you have all sorts of things to do, Mr. Grantland, so we won't ask you to stay." She couldn't bear the idea of his watching her first fumbling attempt at teaching, so she gave him a bright, confident smile, hoping that he would take the hint.

A titter began at the front of the room and swept backward. What had she said that was so funny?

She looked at David and saw amusement in his eyes. Had she made a mistake already?

"Don't worry," he said softly. "It's nothing. Your way of using English just sounds as funny to the children as their way of speaking sounds odd to you. You'll get used to one another."

Christy nodded with relief.

"Sure you don't want me to stay?" he asked. The look in his eyes told her he thought it would be a good idea to let him.

For a moment, staring at the big boys in the back of the room, she wavered.

"Lundy Taylor," David commented, keeping his voice low. He nodded toward a boy as tall as a grown man. He had a sullen expression, as if he were looking for a fight. "He's never been to school before with the Allen children."

"I don't understand."

"There's a feud between the two families," David said. "As old as these hills."

Christy thought for a moment. The boys might cause trouble, and it would be nice to have David nearby for help. On the other hand, last night at dinner Miss Alice had explained that in the mountains, women were still not accepted as equal. It was important, Christy knew, that she deal with this situation herself and make it clear that she was in charge.

"Thank you, David," she said, trying to sound confident. "I'll take it from here."

David nodded. He seemed doubtful, but she could see a glimmer of respect in his eyes. Without another word he left.

Christy took a deep breath. So now she was on her own. All at once the children seemed like giants. She leaned against the edge of the desk for support. A little boy in the front row whispered behind his hand, "She's scared."

"How can ya tell?" Little Burl asked.

"Look at her shakin'."

He was right. Her legs were trembling violently. Christy breathed deep and thought, *Well, it would be best to start at the beginning.* Her first task was to get an attendance roll on paper. She needed to know her students' names and have some information on how much schooling they'd had.

She beckoned to Ruby Mae, a familiar face. She knew Ruby Mae could write some. "Could you and two other girls help me take a roll?"

"Well, yes'm, I reckon so," Ruby Mae said thoughtfully. "What's take a roll?"

"Write down each pupil's name, age, address, and so on. I'll tell you what to do." She pointed to a pretty girl who looked about twelve or thirteen. "Who's that blond girl there? Red bow in her hair?"

"That's Bessie Coburn, my best friend. She's had schoolin' afore."

"She'll do fine. And over there—" Christy spied Clara Spencer, Fairlight's oldest daughter. "How about you, Clara? Would you like to help?"

Clara glowed and jumped from her seat.

"This is a special job, an important one," Christy explained as Ruby Mae puffed with pride. "We want to write down the full name of each pupil." Christy handed each girl a ruled tablet and a pencil. "Age. Beneath that, parents' names . . . home address . . . and schooling the child might have had."

Bessie shook her head. "I vow and declare, Teacher. That 'home address' . . . I'd be much obliged if you'd tell us what you're meanin' by it."

"Where they live. So I can send parents reports and notices and so on. We have to know that."

"Can't guess what she's gettin' at," Ruby Mae said to Clara, who seemed puzzled too.

"Tell you what. Let's each take a row," Christy said. "You watch me with the first name, and then you'll understand perfectly."

All the pupils in Christy's row were boys. The first one looked to be about a second-grader. He was blond, with eyes that looked directly at her as he spoke. He had the firmest mouth she had ever seen on a youngster. "Your name?" Christy asked, her pen poised, ready to write.

"Front name or back name?"

"Well . . . er, both."

"Front name is Sam Houston."

There was a long pause. "A fine name," Christy prodded. "A Tennessee hero. He picked up where Davy Crockett left off, didn't he?" She paused. "Well, now, your—what did you call it—back name?"

"Holcombe."

"Fine. And your father's full name?" Christy asked, writing away.

"He's John Swanson Holcombe."

"And your mother's name?"

"She's just Mama."

"But she has a name. What's her name?"

"Womenfolks call her 'Lizzie.'"

"But her real name?" Christy pressed.

The small brow wrinkled. "Let me study on it now. Oh, surely. Now I know. Elizabeth Teague Holcombe," the boy announced triumphantly.

Christy glanced over at her three helpers. Their faces seemed to say, *You see, not quite as easy as you thought.*

Christy questioned Sam Houston Holcombe. He was nine years old. He had never been to school before. "Last question, Sam," Christy said.

"Generally go by Sam Houston, Teacher."

"Of course. I beg your pardon. And now your address. Tell me where you live."

"Well—" Again, the puzzled look appeared on the small face. "First you cross Cutter Branch. Then you cut across Lonesome Pine Ridge and down. The Gap's the best way. At the third fork in the trail, you scoot under the fence and head for Pigeonroost Hollow. Then you spy our cabin and pull into our place, 'bout two miles or so from the Spencers.'"

Christy scribbled something down quickly, aware of the three girls watching her. Obviously she was going to have to come up with some new system in a hurry for addresses in Cutter Gap.

Slowly she worked her way down the row. Her third student was a boy who claimed his name was Zacharias Jehoshaphat Holt. As soon as the name was out of his mouth, the room burst into snickers.

The boy immediately behind him said softly, "Plumb crazy. That ain't your name at all."

Christy smiled. She recognized the Tom Sawyer look-alike as Creed Allen, one of the boys she'd met at the Spencers' cabin that awful day.

"This isn't the time for fooling," Christy said with just a hint of sternness. "We're trying to get the roll down. Now tell me your real name."

"Zacharias Jehoshaphat—" With that, the boy's right ear jerked violently.

The children laughed uproariously, some of them doubling over. Creed, still straight faced, volunteered, "Teacher, that's not his name. He's packin' lies. You can tell. Just look at his ear."

Sure enough, Zacharias' ear jerked again. "Certainly, I see his ear," Christy said. "But what's that got to do with not telling the truth?"

"Oh, ma'am! All those Holts, when they tell a whopper, their ears twitch—"

Christy ignored him. She turned again to the boy in front. "Tell me your name," she said again.

"Zacharias—" He snickered, then swallowed. "Jehoshaphat—"

Once again, the ear wiggled. But this time Christy saw it—the boy had a string over his ear. With narrowed eyes, she reached over to remove the cord. But Creed jerked it away from her and stuffed the string in his desk.

That did it. Christy knew she had to control the class or this sort of prank would get out of hand. She marched to Creed's desk and reached in. But instead of string, her fingers touched . . . a mass of wriggling fur! She squealed and stepped back, and a small animal as frightened as she was climbed onto the desk, screeching in protest. A ring-tailed raccoon sat there, looking at Christy from behind his funny mask of a face. He began scolding her, as if he were the teacher and Christy were the naughty pupil.

Naturally, the schoolroom fell into chaos—the girls giggling, the boys holding their middles and laughing so hard that one of them got the hiccups.

"Now," Christy said, "let's begin all over." She was trying her best to be patient, but who had ever heard of having this much trouble getting a few names on paper?

"Creed there put me up to it," said the boy who claimed his name was Zacharias. "Said if I'd do it, he'd let me sleep with his coon for one night."

Christy turned to Creed. "This is your raccoon, Creed?"

"Yes'm. Pet coon. Scalawag."

"Might be a good name for you too," Christy commented. She turned to the boy in front of Creed. "All right, now, let's have your real name."

"Front name is Zacharias for a fact, Teacher. You can just call me Zach. That 'Jehoshaphat,' now, that was made up. Back name is Holt. Six of us Holts in school."

At last she was making progress. With some effort, Christy obtained the rest of the information she needed. That brought her back to Creed, whose eyes glittered with—was it intelligence or mischief? Perhaps both. Quickly she decided that she'd better try to make friends this first morning.

"How old is Scalawag, Creed?"

"Got him from a kit last summer."

"What's a kit?"

"Like a nest. He's most grown now. Sleeps with me." Seeing the expression on Christy's face, he added, "Oh, he's clean all right. Coons wash every natural blessed thing before they eat. They're the best pets in the world. Teacher, come spring, maybe we could spy out a kit and get one for you."

"Uh, thanks, Creed. Tell you what. Let me think about that offer. Now, about Scalawag and school—"

"Oh, Scalawag won't cause no trouble. Cross my heart and hope to die."

What could she say without caving in this friendship before it got started? Suddenly Christy had an inspiration. "It's like this, Creed." She lowered her voice. "This is just between you and me. Promise you won't tell?"

"Cross my heart."

"Scalawag is such a 'specially fine coon. I can see that already—you know, so good-looking and such a little comic actor—that the children will want to watch him instead of doing their lessons." She grinned. "How about you and I make a pact? You leave Scalawag home after this. Then I'll let you bring him to the last social, the big recitation just before school closes. We'll fix it so that Scalawag will be part of the entertainment."

"Honest, Teacher?" Creed's face shone. "That's a sealed bargain, fair and square. Why, pretty much everybody in the Cove will see Scalawag then. Put it there, Teacher!" He stuck out a grubby hand.

Well, then. She'd handled that little crisis, at least. Christy gazed around her. Sixty-seven eager faces were waiting for her next move.

It was going to be a very long day.

Eleven

AS THE DAY WORE ON, CHRISTY NURSED A GROWING UNEAS-
iness about the big boy in the back row, the one David had
pointed out as Lundy Taylor. She tried to tell herself that
David had been overreacting, but it was true that the Taylor
boy was uncooperative. He never joined in the singing, never
took part in anything. Resentment of some sort smoldered in
him. Already he seemed to dislike Christy.

There were so many other problems too. The fire in the
stove that was much too hot close to it, much too cold in
the rest of the room. The dripping noses, and the complete
lack of handkerchiefs. The dirty, often smelly clothes, and the
need for warmer ones. The mountain dialect that was almost
impossible for Christy to understand. The fact that children
who wanted a drink went back and forth to the cedar water
bucket in the back of the room, everyone drinking from the
same gourd—a good way to start epidemics.

And then there was the utter lack of books. How was she
supposed to teach sixty-seven students without any materials?

During the noon recess, which the students called "the

dinner spell," Christy sat on the steps, watching the children and wondering how she was going to handle them all. She was surprised when Little Burl came up and sat down beside her like an old friend. He was eating his lunch—a biscuit split in two with a thin slice of pork between the halves.

"I'd be proud to share, Teacher," he said.

"Thank you, Little Burl," Christy said, "but I've already eaten." It wasn't exactly true. Actually, she was simply too anxious to eat.

Just then a pair of black-capped chickadees fluttered to the tree nearest the schoolhouse entrance. Little Burl hesitated, then tossed part of his biscuit to the birds, who swooped down, devouring every last crumb.

"That was nice of you, Little Burl," Christy said, knowing that the boy probably didn't get enough to eat as it was. "They're pretty little birds, aren't they?"

"Eat upside down sometimes, chickadees do," Little Burl said. He shook his head. "Crazy birds."

"Isn't it great how many different kinds of birds there are, each one so special," Christy exclaimed. "God must have cared about them, or He wouldn't have made them so beautiful."

Little Burl thought about this, nodding as he finished his biscuit.

"He loves everything He's made—every bird, every animal, every flower, every man and woman, every single one of you," Christy said. "Loves you extra-specially."

Little Burl didn't answer. Suddenly quiet, he stared off at something only he could see. *I'm trying too hard*, Christy thought. *Will I ever be able to reach these children?*

Just then the background hum of high-pitched voices

was shattered by a screech of pain and then violent crying. Christy ran around the corner, her shoes slipping in the snow.

Vella Holt, a tiny five-year-old with auburn pigtails, was crumpled up on the ground, sobbing. The other children had gathered in a circle around her.

"Has a pump knot on her head," a voice volunteered as Christy took the child in her arms.

The little girl did have a large bump. It was going to be a nasty bruise. What was worse, the blow had been dangerously close to her temple.

"What happened?" Christy asked.

No one answered. Christy looked up. The circle of faces looked too grave, too careful. "Someone has to tell me," Christy persisted. "Did Vella fall down?"

"No'm," Ruby Mae said softly. "She got hit."

"How? With what?"

Someone thrust a homemade ball into Christy's hands. It was so much heavier than she expected that she almost dropped it. It seemed to be made of strips of old cloth wound round and round and then bound with thread. But when she pushed a thumb through the cloth, she found a rock at the center.

"Vella got hit with this?" Christy cried. "No wonder she has a bump on her head! Who threw this?"

Again, the silence. Then, out of the corner of her eye, Christy caught a movement. She turned to see Lundy Taylor and another older boy, Smith O'Teale, slinking into the empty schoolhouse.

"Did Lundy or Smith throw this?"

The children did not say a word, but their eyes told Christy the truth. She felt chilled and frightened. Could either boy have done such a thing on purpose? As she comforted Vella and put cloths wrung out in fresh snow on her bump, Christy struggled with the problem. She decided to make the boys stay after school and get to the bottom of things, rather than talk to them before all the other pupils.

The rest of the day did not go well. To begin with, Christy was running out of ideas. She'd had big plans for lessons, but now it was clear that much of what she'd arranged was impossible with this many mismatched students. She was glad David would be helping with the math and Bible classes in the afternoon.

What subjects had they not touched on today? Penmanship. Happy thought! Christy was proud of her handwriting. It was a nice script. She would enjoy putting some sentences on the blackboard to be copied.

As she headed for the cracked blackboard, she almost stepped on several marbles. Automatically, she stopped to pick them up. But at that moment a child hurled himself toward her in a flying tackle.

"Teacher, don't touch them!" It was Little Burl, hanging onto her arm, shrieking at her.

She was startled by his ferocity. "Why not? I can't leave them on the floor. Someone will step on them and go scooting."

The little boy looked at her, his face flushed and contorted. "Teacher, them marbles are hot. They'll burn you!"

"Hot?" What was he talking about?

Some of the pupils looked embarrassed. Obviously, there was something Little Burl did not know how to explain. In the back of the room, the laughter started again—Lundy Taylor and some of the older boys.

John Spencer, the fifteen-year-old son of Fairlight and Jeb, stepped forward. "Teacher, I'd thank you to let me pick up the marbles for you. Little Burl was afraid you'd burn your fingers. He's right. Them marbles are red hot."

"How'd they get so hot?"

"They was put in the stove, ma'am."

"You . . . Did you . . . ?"

"No, ma'am. Not me. Guess it was just foolery."

Calmly, John took a rag from his pocket, gingerly picked up the marbles one by one, and then left them on the rag on Christy's desk.

This was too much. A low-down prank—ingenious, but mean, almost as bad as the one on the playground. "Look, a prank's a prank," Christy said. "But this wasn't funny. There are tiny children in this room. What if some of them had stepped on red-hot marbles with bare feet? They'd have gotten badly burned. You see, glass holds heat—"

"It sure does," a self-assured masculine voice said from the doorway. "And your teacher's right."

As David strode toward the teacher's desk, Christy realized how drained she was. The marble trick had been one problem too many.

"Recess time for you, Teacher," David said.

Christy smiled gratefully. She hated to admit it, but she was as relieved as any child would be at the end of the school day.

She couldn't wait to leave.

⌒#⌒

The creek was running even faster than it had been the day she'd fallen in. It had warmed up slightly over the week, enough to melt some of the jagged ice that rose like frozen miniature mountains from the stream.

The log bridge swayed like a baby's cradle, back and forth, back and forth, in the steady wind. Here, from the bank of the creek, the scene wasn't nearly as frightening—just a few logs over a stream that glistened in the winter light. It hardly seemed like a likely place to come face to face with death. But then maybe that's how many things were. Up close, things that seemed simple and straightforward could become complicated and frightening.

Coming to Cutter Gap had been like that. She'd known it would be hard, teaching poor children in the mountains. But not this kind of hard. She hadn't bargained for mean students nearly as old as she was. She hadn't counted on sixty-seven barefooted pupils, most of whom had never seen a book in their lives. She hadn't planned for the difficulties she would have in communicating.

She remembered, with a shudder, the pump knot on little Vella's head and the hot marbles on her classroom floor. She certainly hadn't bargained for that kind of meanness.

Christy brushed the snow off a boulder and sat down. She had her diary with her. She'd retrieved it from the mission house before coming here this afternoon. She opened to her list of goals and laughed out loud. Teaching French? Etiquette lessons? What had she been thinking?

She heard footsteps and turned, her heart pounding.

"I'd have thought you'd want to stay as far away as possible from this bridge," David said, laughing as he approached.

"You know what they say: when you fall off, you need to get right back up on the horse."

David frowned. "You didn't cross—"

"No, I'm afraid it may be spring before I cross that bridge again. I think I should let that particular horse thaw out a bit." She moved over, making room on the boulder. "Were you looking for me? I didn't forget a meeting, did I?"

"No. I just happened to notice you when I came out of my bunkhouse to chop some wood. Thought you might need a little moral support."

"Why's that?" Christy asked lightly. Had she done such a bad job that he'd already heard stories from the children?

"First days are always hard. And this is no easy job." David tossed a rock into the stream. It landed with a musical splash, like a tiny fish.

"Somehow I pictured—" Christy hesitated. There was no point in telling him. He'd just laugh.

"Pictured what?" David asked. When she didn't answer, he said, "Let me guess. You thought it would be easy. That the children, all of them, would welcome you with open arms. That they would be poor, but it would be a nice, clean, easy poor, not one that came with ignorance and filth and smells and superstitions and feuds."

Christy met his eyes. They sparkled with humor, but there was something deeper there too. "How did you know?"

"You forget. I haven't been here that long myself. I came to Cutter Gap with lots of high hopes about bringing the Word of God to these people, about changing their lives overnight." He laughed. "I suppose I expected them to be grateful. Instead they've been resentful and slow to accept me. That's when Miss Alice helped me out."

"She did?"

"She told me I couldn't change the world overnight. That this place belonged to the mountain people and that I was the stranger. That it was up to me to understand them, not the other way around."

"And do you?" Christy asked hopefully.

"Nope." David shook his head. "But I'm learning."

"Did you—" Christy gazed up at the bridge, which was shimmering colorfully in the sunlight like an earthbound rainbow. "Did you ever think about going home, giving up?"

"Sure. I think about it every day." David said it lightly, but Christy thought she heard uncertainty too. "Sometimes I wonder if I can ever really be a part of this place, the way Miss Alice is. The way Doctor MacNeill is."

"He told me you were still learning," Christy said.

David rolled his eyes. "I suppose he's right," he said. "Although I might point out that the doc's more than a little set in his ways." He shrugged. "Anyway. Take your time, Christy Huddleston. It will get easier." He stood and touched her lightly on the shoulder.

She was grateful for the warm smile that seemed to come from somewhere deep inside him.

"Oh, by the way, I heard about the incident with Vella."

"I'd planned to talk to Lundy about it—"

"I see you've quickly figured out where the trouble's likely to start. I tried talking to Lundy and Smith myself this afternoon. Couldn't get anything out of them, so I guess we'll just have to keep an eye on things." His face went grave. "I don't want to worry you, especially when you're feeling nervous enough, but Lundy and his friends are bad news. This won't be the only time you'll have to confront them, and next time it may be worse. If that happens, I want you to come to me, understand?"

Christy nodded. But as she watched David trudge back up

the hill, she remembered some advice Miss Alice had given her about taking charge of the classroom. Christy knew she couldn't run to David every time there was trouble.

She gathered up her diary and started to leave. But after a few steps she turned around. Slowly, methodically, she began to search the bank of the creek, hoping she might find the locket her father had given her. She knew it was crazy. The necklace must have caught on something during her fall or broken when she was underwater. It was probably miles down the stream by now, lost forever. Lost forever like her old life. And in its place was the new life she had chosen: a hard, demanding, terrifying, complicated, lonely life in Cutter Gap.

It's an adventure, she told herself. This was what she'd wanted, what she'd dreamed of. She was doing God's work.

But what if I can't do it well enough? a doubting part of her heart asked.

She gazed up at the bridge. She remembered wondering if Bob Allen's accident and her fall off the bridge had been signals that coming here was a mistake. It would be nice to have a sign that she was on the right track, but so far, God had not delivered one.

Christy trudged back and forth along the creek's bank until the sun began to melt behind the farthest blue-black ridge. In her heart, she'd known all along that the locket was lost. So why was it she couldn't seem to stop crying?

Twelve

"You're not eating a thing," Miss Ida scolded the next morning.

"I'm sorry," Christy apologized, staring unhappily at her eggs. "I haven't got much of an appetite this morning."

"Had plenty of one every other morning," Miss Ida grumbled, pulling Christy's plate away.

Christy got up from the table. "I thought I'd go over to the school a bit early this morning to get things ready." *Like myself*, she added silently.

"May I have a word with you, Christy?" Miss Alice asked.

"Of course. If it's about my lesson plans, I know they still need some work—"

"No, no," Miss Alice said, laughing. She gestured to the porch.

They put on their wraps and headed outside. Their breath hung in the air. The sun was just rising and cast a pink glow over the school.

"Have you ever watched a baby learning to walk, Christy?" Miss Alice asked. "He totters, arms stretched out to balance himself. He wobbles and falls, perhaps bumps his nose. Then he puts the palms of his little hands flat on the floor, hikes his rear end up, and looks around to see if anybody is watching him. If nobody is, usually he doesn't bother to cry, just balances himself . . . and tries again."

"I don't understand."

"That baby can teach us. You can't expect immediate perfection in your schoolroom. It's a walk, and a walk isn't static but ever changing. We Quakers say that all discouragement is from an evil source and can only end in more evil. Feeling sorry for yourself is worse than falling on your face in the first place."

Christy felt unexpected tears sting her eyes. "I came here to do God's work," she whispered. "But what if I can't? What if I'm no good at it?"

Miss Alice draped her arm around Christy's shoulders. "So you fall, like that baby. Maybe you even bump your nose. So you're human. Thank God for your humanness!"

Christy took a deep, steadying breath. "I'll try, Miss Alice," she said.

"That's all you can do, child. 'Give, and it shall be given unto you,'" Miss Alice said softly. "You'll see."

Christy squeezed Miss Alice's hand. As she headed off across the boardwalk toward school, she could feel the woman's gaze upon her, warmer than the dawning sunlight peeking over the mountains.

⟵#⟶

The schoolroom was cold, even though David had already started a roaring fire in the potbellied stove. Christy walked back and forth across the empty room, straightening desks, cleaning off the blackboard, fussing and fidgeting. Her heart hammered in her chest. Her hands were shaking like leaves in a breeze.

"Give, and it shall be given unto you," Miss Alice had said. But what if she didn't have enough to give?

She heard the thump of little steps and turned to see Little Burl in the doorway. He was wearing a coat two sizes too big for him. One elbow had been patched a dozen times it seemed. The sleeves were rolled up, yet still his little hands were hidden. His feet, again, were bare. His nose was running.

"Teacher," he said, "I came early."

"You certainly did," Christy said, trying to force lightness into her voice.

"I was a-thinkin' all last night."

Christy sat down in her chair and motioned for Little Burl to join her. He climbed up into her lap. "What were you thinking about, Little Burl?"

"About what you said. About the birds and all."

"The birds?" Christy flashed through yesterday's lessons. Had she mentioned birds? No. Raccoons, yes, but no birds. Well, there you had it. She really wasn't reaching these kids.

"I don't remember about the birds," Christy said gently. "We talked about Creed's raccoon. I remember that—"

"The birds, outside," Little Burl insisted loudly. "The chickadees!"

"Oh, you mean at lunch! The birds you fed. Of course."

Little Burl's funny little face held a look of intense concentration. "Teacher, you said that God loves everybody, right?"

"That's right," Christy said.

"Well, then, ain't it true that if God loves everybody, then we'uns got to love everybody too?"

Christy looked at the little boy in astonishment. "Yes, Little Burl," she encouraged, "it is true." *Forever and forever and forever*, she added silently.

He broke into a smile, relieved. "Thought so."

Christy watched as he scampered back out the door. One comment, an offhand remark during noon recess, had set this little boy to thinking. Something she'd said had mattered. Something she'd said had made a difference.

Perhaps God's work started in small ways.

She'd wanted a sign. Maybe this, after all, was the one she'd been waiting for.

Christy went to the door. The children began to appear as the day broke. In twos, in clumps, dancing, skipping, running, their faces filled with hope and joy. And sometimes, yes, filled with darker things—loneliness, hunger, fear, even anger.

She was surprised when she saw Fairlight Spencer walking toward the school, her children by her side. She was carrying a little leather pouch in one hand. The other held the toddler named Little Guy.

"Fairlight!" Christy exclaimed. Strangely, when Fairlight returned her smile, Christy felt like she was seeing an old, very dear friend.

"I tell you, these children hardly slept a wink last night, they were so excited about school," Fairlight said. She handed the leather pouch to Christy with a shy smile. "John found this a couple days back, over yonder by the bank of the creek."

Christy opened the pouch and reached inside. At the bottom, she felt the cool smoothness of metal.

"My locket?" she whispered.

Slowly she removed the necklace. The chain was gone. In its place was a thin braid of the softest yarn, in blues and greens and blacks and violets.

"I spun and dyed the yarn myself. I know it ain't the same. I sent John and Clara back to look for the chain, but it must have fallen in the creek when you fell in."

Christy grinned. "You heard about that?"

"Word travels fast around these here parts."

"So I hear."

Fairlight peered at Christy, her face lined with worry. "The braidin' is all wrong, I know—"

"It's beautiful," Christy insisted. "More beautiful than before. All the colors of the mountains." Her eyes overflowed with tears. "Thank you, Fairlight. It means more to me than you can know."

Gently, Christy opened the locket. The pictures were damp but unharmed. Her loving family gazed back at her. Christy closed the cover and slipped the braid over her head. She felt the silver heart, close to her own heart again. It was part of her old life. And now, with Fairlight's gift, part of her new one as well.

"Let's start those reading lessons soon, all right?" Christy said.

"I can't hardly wait," Fairlight said eagerly.

Christy nodded. "Neither can I," she said with sudden feeling.

She took a deep breath. The morning sun was full now, a glorious red gold, filtering down through these mountains that were her home.

She felt a tiny, cold hand take hold of hers. "Ready?" Little Burl asked.

Christy smiled down at the little boy. "Did you ever see a baby learn to walk, Little Burl?" she asked. And then, at last, she knew the adventure she had longed for was about to begin.

About Catherine Marshall

Catherine Marshall LeSourd (1914–1983), a *New York Times* bestselling author, is best known for her novel *Christy*. Based on the life of her mother, a teacher of mountain children in poverty-stricken Tennessee, *Christy* captured the hearts of millions and became a popular CBS television series. As her mother reminisced around the kitchen table at Evergreen Farm, Catherine probed for details and insights into the rugged lives of these Appalachian highlanders.

The Christy® of Cutter Gap series, based on the characters of the beloved novel, contains expanded adventures filled with romance, excitement, and intrigue.

Catherine also wrote *Julie*, a sweeping novel of love and adventure, courage and commitment, tragedy and triumph, in a Pennsylvania steel town during the Great Depression.

Catherine's first husband, Peter Marshall, was Chaplain of the U.S. Senate, and her intimate biography of him, *A Man Called Peter*, became an international bestseller and Academy Award Nominated movie. The story shares the power of this dynamic man's love for his God and for the woman he married.

A beloved inspirational writer and speaker, Catherine's enduring career spanned four decades and six continents, and reached over 30 million readers.

CHRISTY'S ADVENTURES CONTINUE IN...

Everybody in the Cove seems to believe that the new school teacher is cursed. Granny O'Teale is determined to drive Christy out of Cutter Gap forever.

Will fear and superstition triumph? Or, will Christy win over the hearts of the mountain people?